This Book Belongs
to....vivianiR

SHE'S the LIAR!

SHE'S -the- LIAR!

Alison Cherry

Scholastic Press / New York

Library of Congress Cataloging-in-Publication Data
Names: Cherry, Alison, author.
Title: She's the liar / Alison Cherry.
Other titles: She is the liar
Description: First edition. | New York: Scholastic Press, 2019. | Summary: Entering Brookside Academy in the sixth grade, Abby is determined to reinvent herself as a confident and popular "Abbi," but she is shocked to find out that her older sister, Sydney (eighth grade), has already crafted a new identity as the president of the "Committee," the all-powerful student organization that controls extracurricular life and rules the student body through intimidation—and inevitably the two clash, because they both know what the other is hiding, and soon they are hopelessly tangled up in the lies they have created for themselves.
Identifiers: LCCN 2018046401 (print) | LCCN 2018049075 (ebook) | ISBN 9781338497144 (ebook) | ISBN 9781338306149 (hardcover)
Subjects: LCSH: Boarding schools—Juvenile fiction. | Sisters—Juvenile fiction. | Identity (Psychology) —Juvenile fiction. | Conduct of life—Juvenile fiction. | Student government—Juvenile fiction. | CYAC: Boarding schools—Fiction. | Schools—Fiction. | Sisters—Fiction. | Identity—Fiction. | Conduct of life— Fiction. Classification: LCC PZ7.C41987 (ebook) | LCC PZ7.C41987 Sh 2019 (print) | DDC 813.6 [Fic]—dc23
LC record available at https://lccn.loc.gov/2018046401

10 9 8 7 6 5 4 3 2 1   19 20 21 22 23

Printed in the U.S.A.   23
First edition, June 2019

Book design by Maeve Norton

CHAPTER 1

The minute my parents leave me alone in my empty dorm room, I stand very still, close my eyes, and let myself disappear.

Just like I've been practicing, I concentrate on my top layer of anxiety first, willing it to waft away like campfire smoke. I force myself to forget that I've never been away from home for more than two nights in a row, that I don't even know where the bathrooms are, let alone the dining hall or any of my classrooms. I let go of the fact that after dinner, my parents are leaving me here at Brookside Academy and driving two whole hours home, across the Vermont state line and back into Massachusetts. I tell myself I'm not nervous to share this room with a complete stranger, a mysterious sixth grader named Christina who has literally five times as many shoes as I do.

When all the surface-level jitters are gone, I reach down deeper and focus on the shyness that has spent so many years wrapped around my bones. I unwind the tendrils that keep me from raising my hand in class even when I know the answers. I find the Abby who sits alone at lunch, nose buried in a book so no one will talk to her, and I let her wither away to ashes. I breathe out the impossibility of making friends with any of my brand-new classmates and breathe in clean, fresh air.

And when Abby is nothing more than a light, empty shell, I let Abbi climb inside me and make herself at home in my skin.

When I open my eyes, I am an entirely different person. Abbi pulls Abby's hunched shoulders back and weaves her tangled hair into a neat side-braid, leaving her face exposed. When I look in the full-length mirror on the back of my closet door, I see Abbi's straight spine, the lift of her chin, the way her hands tuck casually into her pockets like they're resting, not hiding. For all anyone at Brookside knows, I've always been Abbi, confident and relaxed. They'll never know they're looking at the girl who cried in front of the whole school during the third-grade talent show, who accepted zeroes on presentations after that because she couldn't bear to stand in front of a class and face the pity in twenty-five pairs of eyes.

I'm ready to begin my brand-new life.

Turning into Abbi gives me energy, and I start unpacking. Before my parents went to drop Sydney off at her dorm, Mom helped me make my bed with my new green sheets and duvet with the leaf pattern, but all my clothes are still in boxes. I rip open the top one and start unloading my Abbi outfits and

Brookside uniforms. Abbi wears colorful shirts printed with stripes and polka dots and stars when she's not in her kilt and blazer. She's not trying to hide. She even has a few dresses. I stuff all my too-big Abby sweatshirts with the stretched-out sleeves into the back of my bottom drawer, behind my pajama pants. I like knowing they're here, but I don't ever plan on bringing them out.

There's a corkboard hanging over my bed, a group of clear pushpins clustered in the corner. Christina's board is already covered in pictures—a few family photos, a couple of shots of little kids, and a whole bunch of pictures of girls holding tennis rackets, their arms slung casually around one another's shoulders. I don't have any photos to hang, so I tack up a few of the paintings I did this summer: one abstract with swirls of red and orange and gold, another of stark winter trees and flying birds. I hope people will think I'm artistic and mysterious when they see them and not realize I just don't have any friends to photograph.

A key clicks in the lock, and the way my heart jumps into my throat makes my Abbi facade waver like water rippling around a skipped stone. But I breathe slowly and remind myself that Christina doesn't know a single thing about me. She won't ever know anything besides what I choose to tell her. I can be whoever I want here.

The door swings open, and a short girl with a heart-shaped face, light brown skin, and curly black hair takes one step into the room, then freezes at the sight of me. All those shoes made me think she'd be super glamorous, way too cool for me, but she looks totally normal. Actually, to be honest, she looks kind of terrified.

"Oh!" she says. "I didn't know you were . . . I guess you're my . . . Are you Abby?" She immediately starts blushing. "I mean, I guess you must be, or why would you be in here, right?"

Her deer-in-the-headlights expression makes me feel calmer. The more flustered she is, the more collected I'll seem. "Yes, I'm Abbi. Hi." I hold out my hand to her, which feels totally weird—I've never shaken hands with someone my age, or maybe anyone at all. But it seems like something Abbi would do, so I commit to it and force my arm not to tremble.

The girl stares at me, then rushes over and grips my fingers for a second. Her hands are freezing cold and slightly damp. "I'm Christina," she says. "Ha, I guess you knew that already. I hope you don't care that I took the right side? I share with my sister at home and . . . I mean, I was hoping . . ." She lets the sentence trail off and finishes with a shrug.

"I like the left side," I say.

"Oh good," she says, obviously relieved. She plops down on her bed, picks up the stuffed octopus by her pillow like she's considering hiding it, then puts it down again. "Are your parents still here? Mine had to . . . Um, my grandparents came with us, and they had to . . . They left already." She digs the toes of her bright blue sandals into the nubbly industrial carpet.

"Mine are still here," I say. "They're helping my sister move in across campus. She's in eighth grade."

Christina's eyes widen. "You have a sister here? Oh wow.

Did she . . . You probably know how everything works here already."

I don't know how anything works—Sydney has never offered any information, and I don't intend to ask her for it. Actually I plan to make sure our paths cross as little as possible. First of all, she's the only one at Brookside who knows the old me, and I refuse to let Abby crop up and ruin all my plans. And second of all, Syd's not exactly the friendliest person in the world, so I don't want my name attached to hers before people get to know me. I'm pretty sure Mom and Dad thought sending us to the same boarding school would make us closer, but if I have anything to say about it, that is definitely not going to happen. Considering the fact that Sydney barely talked to me even when we lived at home, I think she'd agree.

But Christina doesn't need to know any of that, so I shrug one shoulder and smile. Hopefully it looks modest.

"You're so lucky," Christina says. She pulls the octopus into her lap and winds one of the tentacles around her hand. "Are you guys, like, best friends?"

"No," I say. "We're into different stuff." I don't know how Syd spends her time at Brookside, but before she went, she mostly hid in her bedroom, reading about space and doing a million extra-credit assignments even though she was getting all As. For a long time, her only friends were her Dungeons & Dragons group, and then I guess she had a falling out with them when she was in sixth grade, and Mom and Dad decided boarding school might be a "healthier environment" for her for seventh and eighth grades. I still don't know exactly what happened; when I asked, Syd told me to leave her alone.

Christina nods. "So, do you think you'll do any clubs or sports or anything?"

At my old school I was in Art Club, a safe, quiet place where I could work on my own projects and never speak to anyone. But I feel like maybe I could do something *bigger* now that I'm here. "I'm not sure yet," I say. "I'll go to the activities fair and see what I think. I'm not ready to commit to anything yet. How about you?"

"The tennis team, probably. If I make it, I mean. And . . . I don't know, maybe concert band? Next semester when I'm settled in? I'd like to learn cello." Christina says it quietly, like she's never admitted that out loud before. Maybe she hasn't. Maybe she's creating a new self here too.

"You totally should," I say. "That sounds awesome."

A cheer goes up from outside, followed by a bunch of girls' voices shout-singing about Brookside spirit. Christina hops off the bed and struggles to raise the blinds so we can see what's happening, but they're caught on something and won't go up. She tugs harder, and as the song reaches its climax, the blinds detach from the top of the window frame and come crashing down on Christina's desk. We leap out of the way with identical shrieks as they hit the corner, bend in the middle, and slither to the floor, where they lie like a snake that's been whacked with a shovel.

For a second we both stare at them in horror. Then Christina whispers, "Oh *no*. What do we do?"

Abby wouldn't have known what to do. She probably would've hidden the broken blinds in the back of her closet and gone the whole year without new ones, scared that asking for help would draw unwanted attention. But Abbi doesn't want to change clothes in the bathroom for the next nine months. She's ready to take charge.

"I guess we tell someone we need new ones? The RA, maybe?"

"Do you think we'll get in trouble? Will they give us detention? Classes haven't even started yet." There's a quaver in Christina's voice.

"I don't think so. It was an accident." But my roommate just stares at me, wide-eyed and scared as a baby rabbit, and it makes me say, "Do you want me to go ask?"

She lets out a huge breath of relief. "Would you?"

"Sure. No problem." And weirdly enough, I find that it isn't.

I open the door and step into the hall alone.

Stronger Hall is in complete chaos. Hesitant sixth graders trail behind their parents, lugging suitcases and boxes and looking for their rooms; I wonder which of them will be in my classes. Reunited seventh and eighth graders scream and leap into one another's arms, and I barely avoid being knocked over as a lanky girl barrels out of her room and hugs her friend so hard that they spin all the way around and crash into the wall. My heart tugs painfully toward them the way it always does when I see best friends. But now that I'm Abbi, willing to reach out and talk to other people, a friendship like that might actually be possible for me. I can't wait to find out if it is.

I continue down the hall, past a girl gathering a spilled arm-ful of books and another girl arguing with her dad, until I find the RA's door. I knock, three confident raps. Nobody answers. I knock again, a little louder this time—still nothing. On my third try, a girl comes out of the next room over. She's got pale, freckled skin, long reddish hair, and even longer knee socks patterned with stars. "Are you looking for Amelia? I think she took someone to the infirmary."

"Oh," I say. It's not a big deal, but it's hard not to be disap-pointed. I really wanted to burst back into our room and assure Christina that I handled everything, all Abbi-to-the-rescue.

"Maybe I can help?" says the girl.

She looks about Sydney's age, which means she actually might know the answer to my question. "The blinds in our room broke," I say. "Do you know how we get new ones?"

"Oh, the Committee handles that."

I blink at her. "The . . . what?"

"Oh, sorry, you're new, aren't you? The Brookside Academy Student Representative Officers Committee? We call them the Committee 'cause BASROC sounds super dumb. Brookside's really big on the students running everything. So if you need something repaired, or if you want to reserve a room or get money for your club or throw an event or something, all of that goes through them."

"Huh." This is a lot more complicated than I was expecting—I thought I could just tell the RA and someone would magically bring us new blinds. "So, I have to, what, email them?"

The girl laughs like I've suggested I sing my request through a megaphone from the top of Memorial Church. "No, you go to Petition Day and ask for what you want."

I've only been a Brookside student for two hours, but she says it like it's totally obvious. Maybe it is. Maybe I missed something important in the welcome packet. I don't want to look more clueless than I already do, so I say, "Okay, thanks. I'll get my sister to explain how it works."

"Oh, you have a sister here? What's her name?"

I consider lying. But people are going to figure out that Sydney and I are related eventually, and being caught in a lie first thing is worse than being associated with her. So I say, "Sydney? She's in eighth grade."

The girl's eyes get big. "*Sydney*'s your sister? Really?"

My heart speeds up at the expression on her face. "Yeah?" I brace myself to hear something about how weird my sister is, how she acts like a know-it-all and alienates everyone like she did at our old school. I desperately hope that saying her name hasn't destroyed my chances of being cool, glamorous Abbi.

But the girl just says, "So you know all about the Committee already!"

Like Christina, she obviously assumes that Sydney has taught me what to expect here; most big sisters probably would have. I force a laugh, which comes out higher and more musical than my regular laugh; I guess this is how Abbi laughs. "Oh, it's *that* Committee?" I say. "Of course. I forgot for a second. Thanks."

The redhead is staring at me now like I've become five hundred times more interesting in the last ten seconds. "I'm sure *you'll* never have any trouble getting what you want," she says. "What's your name?"

"Abbi," I say. "With an *i*."

"Hi, Abbi-with-an-*i*. I'm Grace. It's really nice to meet you. Do you think maybe you could put in a good word for me with the Committee?"

I'm not sure why explaining things to a sixth grader would get her special privileges with the Committee, but I'm happy to tell them how helpful she's been, so I say, "Sure. It's nice to meet you too. See you around?"

"See you," says Grace, and she disappears back into her room. I can hear her talking excitedly to her roommate, but I can't understand what she's saying.

As I turn and make my way back to my room, I break into a smile. I didn't accomplish what I came out here to do; I have no answers for Christina, and I'm actually a lot more confused than I was five minutes ago. But I had a perfectly normal interaction with a stranger, and I didn't freak out even when I couldn't follow the conversation. I bet Grace had no idea I was even nervous.

It turns out Abbi's an excellent actress. It makes me wonder what other skills she might have.

CHAPTER 2

The dining hall is having a welcome dinner for students and their parents, and I'm torn about whether it's a good idea to go. On one hand, I want to start making new friends in my class right away; Christina and I have already bonded a little over the blinds incident, and I can tell that one tiny strand of similarity or shared experience can tie people together for good here. I want to see who else Abbi can bond with, plus I don't want to leave Christina to fend for herself. The way she looks at me like I can handle anything makes me feel more competent than I ever have in my life.

But at the same time, I don't want anyone to meet me for the first time while I'm sitting next to my sister. I'd rather people see me walking between the tables in my brand-new clothes with my mysterious Abbi smile and think, *Who's* that *girl?*

Where did she *come from?* If Syd's there, she'll ruin everything with the sulky, know-it-all attitude that wafts off her like some kind of horrible perfume. The fewer people who figure out we're related, the better.

I'm not sure how to tell my family I'd rather go somewhere else to eat; my parents are awesome, and I don't want them to think I'm embarrassed to be seen with them. But it turns out Sydney takes care of the problem for me. When I meet the three of them in front of my dorm, the first thing she says is, "Can we go off campus for dinner?"

Mom reaches out to smooth my sister's hair, and she doesn't even look hurt when Syd wriggles away; we're all used to how prickly she is. "It's your first night back," Mom says. "Don't you want to see your friends?"

"We'd love to meet some of them," Dad says. He's wearing a dorky BROOKSIDE DAD hoodie, and it makes him look ridiculous and adorable all at once.

Syd squirms and looks down, rubbing her left eye behind her glasses the way she always does when she's nervous, and I actually feel bad for her. It's totally possible she's all alone here, like we both were at our old school, and she doesn't want Mom and Dad to know. I'd be embarrassed too if I were her. I'm definitely not going to let that happen to me this time around.

"Can we get pizza or something?" she asks. "We're going to have to eat dining hall food every single night all year."

"I thought you said the dining hall food was great," Dad says, but Mom puts her hand on my sister's back and says,

"If that's what you want, it's fine." She turns to me. "Is that okay with you, though, Abby? It's your first night at Brookside, and we want to make sure you feel comfortable. If you'd rather go to the dining hall to see how things work . . ."

Old Abby probably would've been nervous about the dining hall, about not knowing where to get a tray or how fast cereal comes out of the dispenser or how many cookies you can take before people look at you weird. But now that I'm Abbi, I'm pretty sure I can learn by watching the other girls. If I make mistakes, I'll just laugh them off, and maybe nobody else will think they're a big deal either.

"It's fine if Syd wants pizza," I say. "I'm sure I can figure out the dining hall tomorrow. I'll get my roommate to show me."

My parents exchange the kind of look where you can practically see words flying back and forth between their brains. They're obviously surprised by my new attitude, but it's like they decide together not to mention it. "Okay," Dad says, clapping his hands. "Pizza it is."

We end up at a place called Stromboli about ten minutes from campus. Syd seems to relax as we settle in at a table with a red-and-white-checkered cloth and order drinks. But then the door opens again, and when three other girls walk in with their parents, her whole posture changes, shoulders flying up to her ears like she wishes she could retract her head like a turtle. The girls all look perfectly nice, and one of them even waves and calls, "Hi, Sydney!" But my sister just gives them a tight smile. Maybe they're mean girls who are pretending to be sweet in front of their families.

"Oh, are those friends of yours?" my mom asks. "If you want to eat with them, maybe we could get the waiters to move some tables together and—"

"No," Syd says, and her voice comes out so low and dangerous that Mom breaks off right in the middle of her sentence.

"Oh," she says, looking a bit bewildered. "Well . . . okay."

"See you Tuesday!" calls another girl as the server leads them to their table. She's wearing a pink shirt so bright it almost hurts to look at it. "We have some really amazing ideas for the dance team this year, and we're hoping you'll—"

Syd's hand shoots out of her lap quick as lightning, and her Sprite topples and splashes all over the table like a bubbly waterfall. Mom and I yelp and scoot out of the way as soda pours in streams off the tablecloth, ice cubes riding on top like tiny rafts. A server comes to the rescue with extra napkins right away, and by the time everything is cleaned up, the girls and their parents are seated all the way across the restaurant.

"Oops," Sydney says, but she doesn't apologize or anything. It kind of seems like she did it on purpose to end the conversation.

Something the girl in pink said tugs at the corner of my brain as I reach for a garlic knot. "You're not on the dance team, are you?" I ask my sister. I can't picture that at all.

"Ew, no!" Sydney snaps, so indignant it's like I've told the whole school who she has a crush on. "I would never associate with those idiots. God, don't be *stupid*."

Syd has never exactly been the warmest, fuzziest sister, but I'm not used to her calling me names, and hearing the word "stupid" directed at me stings like getting a paper cut between my fingers.

"Sydney, *please* be nice to Abby," Mom says.

"Sorry," Syd mumbles.

"That girl said she'd see you Tuesday, though," I say. "What happens Tuesday?"

"Nothing," Syd says. "I don't know. Class, I guess? I barely know her."

I don't know why I even try with her sometimes. I'm about to give up when I remember I actually have an important question. "Oh, hey," I say. "I wanted to ask you—what's Petition Day?"

My sister's eyes widen. "What? Why? Who said anything about Petition Day?"

"Our blinds fell down earlier, and when I asked this girl on my hall how we get new ones, she said I had to go to Petition Day and ask the Committee. And she made it sound like it was obvious what those things were, and I didn't want to look dumb, so I said I'd ask you."

Syd's hand flies up to rub her eye again; it's lucky she doesn't wear makeup, or she would look like a raccoon by now. "Okay," she says, a little calmer. "So, the Committee is made up of six students, two from each grade. Well, there are four right now, since elections for sixth-grade representatives aren't for another few weeks, but soon there'll be six. It's like student council, but they have a lot more control over what happens at the school. They meet every day during first period, and then they also have Petition Days on Tuesday and Friday afternoons. If you need something, you go to the Student Government Office in the basement of the Student Center, and you fill out a form. And then you stand in line to go before the Committee and ask for what you need. If it's something quick, they vote on it right then—like, I'm sure your blinds will get approved right away. If it's bigger, like you want money for your club or something, they wait till their meeting the next morning to discuss it, and then they vote."

"Do you know the girls on it?" I ask. "Are they cool?"

My sister shrugs. "Everyone knows everyone here. I'm not really friends with them or anything."

"I love how progressive this school is," Mom says. "It's so great that you girls get to govern yourselves. It's setting you up to be amazing leaders. I wish I'd had those kinds of opportunities when I was your age. Even just electing your own representatives is such great practice for being a politically engaged adult."

"Yeah, I guess," Syd says.

Our server shows up with our food, and the conversation stops for a minute while we figure out where the Hawaiian pizza and the pepperoni and mushroom and the salad should go. Once everyone is served, Dad says, "How are you feeling about starting school, Abby? Are there any extracurriculars you think you might want to try?"

"I'm sure this school has a wonderful art club," Mom says super gently, like she's tiptoeing toward a sleeping cat and is afraid of startling it. "But do you think it might be cool to try something where you can be part of a team? I played soccer and sang in the choir in middle school, and both of them were such great experiences."

"I did band, and I loved it," Dad says. "I played—"

"Ugh, Dad, we all know about your saxophone," Syd says with a giant eye roll, and everyone laughs. Sometimes on holidays, Dad digs out his saxophone and tries to play it. The only thing he can play is "Jingle Bells," and even that is almost unrecognizable.

"Seriously though, Abs," Mom says. "What do you think?"

I bet Mom thinks I'm going to go quiet, shake my hair down over my face like a curtain, and say I don't want to be part of a team. She has no idea that Abbi's living inside me now, and I can't wait to surprise her with the idea that took root this afternoon and has been growing and flowering ever since.

I sit up straight and put my pizza down; it seems like my big announcement will hold more weight if I don't have sauce all over my fingers. "Actually . . ." I draw the word out, then pause to create suspense, and it works—pretty soon my whole family has stopped chewing and is looking at me. "I think I'm going to try out for the play."

Saying the words out loud makes me feel fizzy with nervous excitement. I love to sing and act in the privacy of my bedroom, and part of me has always wished I could show other people what I could do. After the third-grade talent show, I felt like that door had closed in my face forever. Later that week, when I stood up to give a class presentation about penguins, Evan Hamilton started fake crying, making these loud "Boooo-hooooo" sounds, and everyone in the whole class laughed. And then people started doing it in the lunchroom and on the playground and in the halls, and that's when I basically went quiet for the rest of elementary school. But here I have an audience that doesn't know anything about me, and a brand-new personality to go with it. Abbi can obviously do things I can't do, and it seems like this might be one of them.

"Abby, that's . . ." Mom's voice wavers, and her eyes go all soft and warm, like a caramel that's been sitting in the sun. "Sweetheart, that's a wonderful idea. I'm so proud of you."

Dad reaches out and squeezes my hand. "I can't wait to see my girl onstage."

Sydney looks back and forth between my parents like they've said they're going to get a pet ostrich and keep it in her bedroom. "You guys all know this is a really bad idea, right? We do have a good art club, Abby. You should just be in that, okay?"

"I can be in both," I say.

"But there's no way you can possibly be in the play," Syd says, and her words send little sparks of doubt showering through me.

Mom shoots my sister a look like she's seriously trying her patience. "Sydney," she says, her voice deadly serious, "could you *please* try to be supportive? Your sister is being really brave, and we think it's wonderful that she wants to try something new. I know that coming back here after a summer at home is an adjustment for you, but Abby's starting at Brookside for the first time, and she's probably more nervous than you are. All our attention can't be on you today."

"What, you think I'm *jealous* of her?" Syd snaps.

"You're the big sister," Dad says. "We need you to act mature and show Abby some kindness, okay?"

"That's not—*augh*." Syd's face is turning red, and she balls up her napkin like there's a bug in the middle that she needs to squish. No matter what she says, I know this *is* about jealousy. My sister has noticed there's something different about me, and she knows I might actually be able to succeed here in a way she hasn't managed. I bet she's afraid I'll get more popular in a week than she's gotten in an entire year. And if all goes well, maybe I will.

I sit up straight and tell myself not to listen to her. She can be unsupportive all she wants. If she believes I can't do it, fine. None of that has to affect me.

I'm going to get up on that stage, and I'm going to show her how wrong she is.

CHAPTER 3

The basement of the Student Center is already crowded with girls by the time I get there after class on Tuesday. Most of them are grouped around a folding table near the vending machines, and when I make my way over, I see that they're jockeying to grab pastel papers from a bunch of plastic trays. These must be the forms Sydney mentioned. Other girls are chatting as they fill them out, sprawled on the squishy, mismatched couches covered in cat scratches and stains. It looks like all the teachers' reject furniture has ended up down here, but it's kind of cozy in a way.

I'm not 100 percent comfortable being Abbi yet, and my stomach twists when I think about pushing into the fray and trying to figure out which form I need. Old Abby would have been terrified of making a fool of herself. But I've done a great job of being Abbi today—I answered questions in math *and* English, and I even made a joke at lunch that Christina and two other girls laughed at. I can totally do this.

I recognize the girl who was wearing the pink shirt at the pizza place on Sunday, so I move toward the table and tap her on the shoulder. "Hi," I say in my perky, confident Abbi voice. "Do you know which form I need to get new blinds for my room?"

The girl grabs a pale blue paper from a tray and passes it back to me. It says MAINTENANCE REQUEST across the top. "Here."

"Thanks," I say, and I smile at her. I'm still getting used to smiling for real in public places; it makes my teeth feel naked and shy. The girl smiles back, so I guess I don't look totally weird, but it definitely doesn't seem like she recognizes me from the other night.

"Is this your first Petition Day?" she asks. I nod, and she says, "When you're done filling out your form, get in line over there, in front of the Student Government Office." She indicates a hallway next to a bulletin board plastered with flyers for clubs and activities; there are at least fifteen girls over there already, a sea of navy blazers and plaid skirts and ponytails. "Don't worry, it usually moves pretty fast."

"Thanks," I say again. "Do they, um . . ." Abbi doesn't say "um," so I swallow and try again. "Does the Committee usually give people what they want?"

"I'm sure you'll have no problem getting new blinds. You'll be in and out in two seconds. But stuff like this . . ." She holds up her yellow form, which says BUDGET REQUEST FOR ACTIVITY.

"I'm not sure what's going to happen. The new president doesn't like me very much, so . . ."

"Does that matter?" I ask. "Even if you're asking for something reasonable?"

The girl shrugs. "With her it does."

"She sounds kind of mean," I say. "I hope you get what you want."

"Thanks. You too."

I find an empty chair in the corner of the room and fill out my form—name, ID number, room number, maintenance issue—and then I get in line. The door of the Student Government Office opens right at that moment, and a girl with curly blond hair and a round face storms out, cheeks red and eyes murderous. A green form is crumpled in her hand. A tall girl with her hair in tons of tiny braids goes inside and shuts the door behind her.

"She said *no*," the blond girl says when she reaches her friends. "Can you believe that? All I'm asking for is two hours off campus so I can go shoe shopping with my mom!"

"That's *so stupid*," says one of her friends. "Did she say why?"

"She said they weren't issuing off-campus passes this early in the year, but she gave one to Brianne ten minutes ago for her sister's birthday party. She's obviously trying to get back at me because I campaigned for Chelsea."

"Chelsea deserved to be president so much more," says a third girl.

"*So* much more. She would've actually run things *fairly*." The girl tips her head back and makes a frustrated, strangled screaming sound. "Gianna and Lily and Maya all wanted to give it to me—I could tell. Like, they were raising their hands to say yes, but then *she* gave them this look, and they all put their hands down. There's a *hole* in the sole of my sneaker. How am I going to do cross-country tryouts?"

"I'm sorry," the first friend says. "You can appeal on Friday, I guess?"

"Tryouts are Thursday. It'll be too late by then."

The door opens again, and the girl with the braids comes out, clutching her yellow form and beaming. She practically skips over to the stairs, where her friend is waiting. "She said they'd consider the telescope!" she says. "They're going to vote on it tomorrow. Can you believe it? I thought for sure they'd say no."

Her friend jumps up and down and squeals. "Oh my god, if we ordered it tomorrow, Astronomy Club could have it by next week for the supermoon! And Saturn is supposed to be so bright the week after—do you think we'd be able to see the rings? We could get so many more people to join."

"Maybe! I'll check the specifications to see—" They head up the stairs, and the slamming door swallows the end of her sentence.

The blond girl's eyes bug out of her head as she watches them go. "Are you *serious* right now? Jenna gets a freaking *telescope*, and I can't have two hours at the mall? I *hate* this place."

Her friend puts an arm around her shoulders. "Let's go get a hot chocolate." They follow the other girls up the stairs.

I guess Dance Team Girl wasn't kidding about the new

president. When I try to picture her, I imagine Maleficent from *Sleeping Beauty*, complete with the horn headdress, the cape, and the raven on her shoulder. I know that's not what the president will look like, obviously—she's an eighth-grade girl, not an evil queen. But my heart gives an anxious flutter anyway, like a scared bird has gotten trapped inside it. It doesn't help when another girl storms out of the room with a giant dark cloud hanging over her head. As she pushes by me, muttering to herself, she crumples her form into a ball and throws it in the trash.

There are just two more people in front of me, and then, after a shockingly short time, there's only one. And then I'm face-to-face with the door of the Student Government Office, and my pulse is so out of control that I can feel it in my fingertips.

I remind myself that I'm only asking for blinds; Sydney and Dance Team Girl both said I'd have no trouble getting them. The president has nothing against me. She's never even seen me before. If I make a good impression, maybe I'll end up like Telescope Girl and I'll be able to get anything I want for the rest of the year.

I take a deep breath, lift my chin, and try to banish every leftover molecule of Abby from my body. And then the girl behind me impatiently says, "It's your turn," and I skitter forward before I'm totally ready, and then I'm inside the room, clutching my blue paper in my clammy fingers.

I close the door behind me and turn to face the Committee.

And then my mouth drops open. Because there behind the table, flanked by three other girls, is my sister.

Her chair is different from their plain metal folding ones; it's wood, with a higher back and arms, and it makes her a bit taller than everyone else. In front of her are a red ink pad and three rubber stamps: APPROVED, DENIED, and PENDING. Not only is Sydney *on* the Committee, it looks like she's *running* it. My sister is the evil queen.

"Syd?" I say, and my voice comes out squeakier than Abbi's ever would. But nobody hears me because Sydney starts talking right over me.

"Hello," she says, totally cool and neutral, like she's never seen me before in her life. "How can we help you today?"

I can't wrap my mind around the fact that my *sister*—my nerdy, know-it-all sister who had to switch schools because she had so much trouble interacting with people—is the dreaded president everyone fears. And she just spent an entire summer at home without ever once mentioning it. Why would she hide something so important from her own family? Why didn't she tell us at dinner on Sunday when I asked about the Committee? And why is she acting like she has no connection to me at all, like we haven't spent practically every day of our lives under the same roof?

I stare at her, stunned into silence by the number of conflicting feelings flooding through my brain, and she stares right back. She's sitting up straight and tall, filled with a fierce confidence I've never seen in her before, and she has this giant pair of lace-up black boots on. They look like the ones she described that time she told me what her Dungeons & Dragons character, Capriana the Rogue, looked like.

"Helloooo?" The girl on Syd's left grabs a handful of cereal out of the Ziploc bag she's holding and stuffs it into her mouth. "Can we have your petition?"

"Um, yeah." I force a smile, hoping I look way more relaxed than I feel. "Here you go." I approach the table and lay the maintenance request form down in front of my sister. It's crumpled along the edge from my sweaty fingers, and I try to smooth it flat.

Syd picks up the sheet, and her eyebrows furrow for a second; she's probably noticing that I've changed the spelling of my name. I wonder if she's going to mention it, but instead she just reads aloud: "Abbi Carrington, sixth grade, Stronger Hall #213."

"Wait, Carrington?" asks the girl to Syd's right. She's got super shiny black hair and a gold dragon pin on the lapel of her blazer. "Are you guys related?"

"Yes," Sydney says, but she doesn't elaborate or even look up from the paper. I know I made plans to distance myself from her at this school, but I never thought she'd try to do the same to me. *I've* never been the problem.

She keeps reading. "Maintenance request to replace broken blinds. All in favor?"

The other three girls watch my sister, obviously hesitant to vote until they see what she's going to do. When Sydney raises her hand and says, "Aye," all three of them echo her immediately. It's like there's a master puppeteer in the ceiling, pulling their marionette strings in unison.

Does the Committee *always* do exactly what Syd wants, no

questions asked? How did she possibly make that happen? Maybe it's because my request was such an easy one. I'm sure they all would've voted yes no matter what; there's no reason to deny a request for *blinds*.

Then again, there's no reason to deny a request for a sneaker-shopping trip either.

"The motion passes," Syd says. She picks up a rubber stamp, seesaws it over her ink pad, and stamps a big red APPROVED on my form. "Take this to the Building Management Office—it's on the first floor of Kemmerling Hall—and give it to Ms. Moskowitz. She'll get you new blinds."

I take the form. "Thanks. But Syd—"

"Thank you for coming in," Sydney says without even a hint of warmth. "Please send the next girl in." And then she looks past me at the door, like she's trying to let me know I'm dismissed.

I thank the other girls and say goodbye, and then I'm back out in the hall, my thoughts crashing and churning like waves breaking against rocks. *This* is why that girl Grace on my hall was so excited that I was Sydney's sister, why she acted like I had an automatic in with the Committee. This is why she thought I was special. But judging from the cold, formal way my sister just treated me, it doesn't seem like I actually have any power at all.

CHAPTER 4

A couple of days ago, I never would've sought my sister out in the dining hall on purpose. But now I scour the room for Sydney at dinner, desperate to ask how this whole Committee president thing happened. Unfortunately she never appears, and she doesn't respond to any of my texts either. I spend the whole evening thinking about it as I try to concentrate on my social studies and Spanish homework, then as I'm falling asleep to the sound of Christina's even breathing. But no matter how many theories I come up with, I can't for the life of me figure out how the Sydney I know—or the Sydney I *knew*, I guess— has managed to become the most powerful person on the Brookside campus. I barely ever saw her *talk* to another kid at our old school, much less be in charge of something.

And by the next morning, I have other things on my mind.

Auditions for the fall play, *Cinderella*, are happening this afternoon.

As I get dressed and weave my hair into Abbi's signature side-braid, old, familiar doubt starts to creep up from the pit of my stomach. I've never been able to do something like try out for a play before, so why would I assume I can do it now? Maybe this is the worst idea I've ever had. But I remind myself that I've been in character since Sunday; I've barely broken once, which means that I really am a great actor. Now that I'm Abbi, I've already accomplished tons of things that Abby never could've managed.

"I'm exhausted," Christina says as we walk to breakfast. "I'm so nervous about tennis tryouts that I barely slept last night."

I've been way more tired than usual lately too—pretending to be outgoing all the time takes so much more energy than hiding behind my hair and keeping my thoughts to myself. But of course I can't tell Christina that, so I instead I say, "You're going to do *amazing*." She told me last night as we brushed our teeth that she's been playing since she was in third grade. "I bet you're already the best player in the sixth grade. I bet you're the best in the entire school."

Christina blushes and looks at the ground. "I mean, I don't . . . Well, thanks. Play auditions are today too, right? How do you . . . Are you scared?"

"It's not that big of a deal," I say with all the Abbi cool I can manage. "I just have to sing a few lines of any song I want and read a little bit. Easy-peasy." And amazingly the moment the words are out of my mouth, it *does* start to feel easier.

"You're so brave," Christina says. "When do you find out if you're in?"

"Right after classes tomorrow, I think."

"Same here," Christina says. "Hey, maybe . . . Would you want to hang out and do something tomorrow night? We could ask . . . Maybe Amelia would let us use the kitchen and make cookies or something? We could celebrate if we get in or, like, stuff our faces with sugar if we don't. Or whatever."

And suddenly it's not just my attitude about the audition that feels different; *everything* feels different. I was invited to birthday parties and stuff at my old school, but only the ones where the whole class came. It's been years since I've had a friend who wanted to celebrate with me, specifically.

"Yes," I say. "Definitely. That sounds awesome." Christina gives me a shy smile, and I think about those two girls on the first day who spun around so hard they crashed into the wall. I wonder if that'll be us next year.

The day goes by in a snap, and before I know it, I'm sitting in the auditorium, clutching my audition sheet and a few stapled pages of a script in my hand. A pretty woman with turquoise streaks in her hair and a colorful scarf around her neck gets up onstage and introduces herself as Ms. Gutierrez.

"I'll be directing this production," she says. "I know some of you already from drama class, but I'm delighted to see some new faces as well." I swear she smiles right at me when she says it, and it feels like a sign that my audition is going to go well.

She points out the music director, Ms. Solomon, and the student assistant director, Grace O'Connor. When she waves,

I realize she's the girl who asked me to put in a good word for her with the Committee. I wonder if that'll help me get into the play even if my audition doesn't go that well.

"I'll call you up in the order you signed in today," Ms. Gutierrez says. "When I call your name, bring me your audition sheet, then come stand right here on this X." She taps the spot on the stage marked with yellow tape with the toe of her shiny blue shoe. "Tell us your name and what grade you're in, then go ahead and sing a few lines of your song. If I tell you to stop, it doesn't mean you're doing badly, it just means we've heard enough to make a decision. Then we'll have you read— your lines are the highlighted ones, and Grace and Ms. Solomon will read the other parts. Does anyone have any questions?"

Nobody does, so Ms. Gutierrez calls the first name on the list, a girl named Kiara. She plants herself on the X and smiles at the audience with so much cool, serene confidence that looking at her makes *me* feel calmer. When she starts to sing, the girl next to me leans over and whispers, "Oh my god, she's *so* good." She sounds totally dismayed.

I nod—Kiara *is* ridiculously good. Her voice is clear and sweet and strong, wrapping around me like a blanket, and she doesn't even look like she's trying. Ms. Gutierrez lets her sing two whole verses before she cuts her off.

The girl next to me leans toward me again as Kiara starts reading Cinderella's lines. I think I recognize her from my algebra class. "Are you nervous?" she asks. "I'm so, *so* nervous." She's twisting the hem of her skirt around her finger so tightly I'm afraid she might rip it.

I give her a little one-shoulder shrug. "It'll be okay. She's super talented, but that doesn't mean we're not talented, you know?"

"Hmm. Yeah. I guess." The girl sits back, and when her grip on her kilt loosens, I feel better too. Turns out Abbi has pretty good advice.

I was the eighth person to sign in, so it doesn't take long before it's my turn. A shot of nerves zings through me when Ms. Gutierrez calls my name, making my insides hum, but I bury those feelings under Abbi's confidence like I'm smothering a fire with sand. Abbi knows she's good at singing, and she's excited to show everyone what she can do. I scoot past the other girls and out of the row, hand over my audition sheet, and make my way up onto the stage and toward the X, my strides long and purposeful. I plant my feet shoulder-width apart, smooth my braid over my shoulder, and force my mouth into a big smile.

As I gaze back at the rows upon rows of eyes staring at me, I feel those old tendrils of terror creeping out of my heart, wrapping around my lungs and my stomach and the animal part of my brain that makes you want to run from predators. This is exactly the view I had the day of that horrible, fateful talent show that sent me scuttling into my shell for more than two years. What if the same thing happens today? What if I break down again? What if everyone at Brookside spends the rest of middle school judging me and laughing at me?

For a moment, I look out into the audience and see thirty Evan Hamiltons making exaggerated crybaby faces and going *Boooo-hooooo!*

But it only takes a moment before Abbi's back in control. There's no chance I'll break down today. I'm in a totally different place. Most of these girls have no idea who I am, and the rest have only known me a few days. They're looking at me with curiosity, not malicious glee. And most importantly I'm a different person now than I was at that third-grade talent show. Abbi would never cry onstage. All I have to do is embody her, sing a song I've practiced a million times, and read some lines off a paper. Like I told Christina, it's easy.

I take a deep breath and say, "Hi, I'm Abbi Carrington. I'm in sixth grade."

"Welcome to Brookside, Abbi," says Ms. Gutierrez with a warm smile. "You can go ahead whenever you're ready."

I close my eyes and take a moment to pull myself together. And then I open my mouth and sing.

I've chosen "How Far I'll Go" from *Moana*, and since I only get a few lines, I go straight to the chorus. It doesn't sound exactly like it did when I practiced alone in my room; the remains of my nerves still cling to me, making me start a little too high, sing a little too fast. But my voice carries all the way to the back of the auditorium, and I hit all the notes. Ms. Gutierrez lets me get through four lines before she says, "Thank you, Abbi. Very nice."

Did she say "very nice" to the other girls? I wasn't paying attention, but it seems like a good sign regardless, so I smile and say thanks. "Are you ready to read?" she asks me.

The pages I have are from a scene between Cinderella and the stepsisters. When I nod, Grace reads the first line, and we're off. I can't even remember the last time I read anything aloud to a room full of people; I've always tried my best to avoid it. But today I don't trip over a single word, and I'm able to concentrate on making myself sound like Cinderella, sweet and sad and overwhelmed with the injustice of being kept from the ball. I expect it to be hard, layering another character over Abbi, being both of them at the same time. But being Abbi quiets the tornado of anxious thoughts that always used to swirl at the back of my brain, leaving room for other things, and it actually makes it easier to slip into someone else's skin.

"Good job, Abbi," says Ms. Gutierrez when I reach the end of the second page. "Would you mind reading the scene one more time, only this time you'll do Portia's lines?"

"Sure," I say, and to my surprise, I find that I don't want this audition to be over. I'm actually *excited* to stay up here longer. Grace reads the first line again, and when it's my turn, I put on a dramatic, whiny evil stepsister voice, hamming it up for everything I'm worth. And when a wave of giggles sweeps through the girls in the audience, I know beyond a shadow of a doubt that they're not laughing *at* me. They're laughing because I'm funny.

The scene goes by way too quickly. Ms. Gutierrez is grinning when she thanks me and tells me I can sit back down, and I float to my seat, every nerve in my body singing with adrenaline and pride. It was one thing for my Abbi self to do normal things like talking in class and petitioning for new blinds; everyone here can do things like that. But not everyone can do what I just did. Abbi is legitimately talented. She rocked that audition.

If I can do this, I can do *anything*.

The moment I slip back into my seat, Skirt-Twisting Girl grabs my arm. Her nails are painted with blue glitter. "Oh my god," she whispers. "Abbi, right? You were *so* good. No wonder you weren't nervous."

"Thank you," I say. "I'm sure you're going to be amazing too."

"I love 'How Far I'll Go,'" the girl says. "I sang it in the shower for like a month straight after I saw *Moana*. It drove my parents bananas."

"Me too," I say, and she smiles.

"I have that movie on my computer—would you maybe want to watch it sometime? I live in Stronger. I'm Lydia, by the way."

"Definitely," I say. "I'm in Stronger too. My roommate and I were actually going to make cookies after dinner tomorrow—do you want to come?" I have to work hard to make my mouth form the words; it's the first time I've asked someone at Brookside to hang out with me, and I'm not sure I can handle being rejected.

But Lydia breaks into a huge smile and says, "Yeah, of *course*! That sounds super fun."

It's only my fourth day of being Abbi, and I've already made more friends than I did in the last two years combined.

CHAPTER 5

It's nearly impossible to concentrate in class the next day, and I can tell there are a bunch of other girls who feel the same—there were a lot of tryouts yesterday. By last-period social studies, there's so much squirming and nail-biting and whispering that Ms. Patrick gives up on talking about ancient Egypt and lets us go five minutes early.

I sprint across the quad to the auditorium, my backpack thumping against my shoulder blades. Until yesterday, even *trying out* for a play seemed like too high a mountain to scale. But now that I've succeeded and I'm on the other side, I can see a whole series of other beautiful peaks in front of me, inviting me to climb them. Rocking the audition isn't enough anymore. I want to stand onstage in front of a packed audience with my Abbi face on, totally in control, making everyone laugh and applaud and feel things. I want that bubbly, floaty feeling back, like fancy sparkling water is coursing through my veins.

I make it to the auditorium as the bell rings for the end of eighth period and girls burst out of the buildings all around me. Someone calls my name over the clamor, and I turn to see Lydia barreling toward me. She's in such a hurry that she hasn't even put her backpack on properly and it's swinging wildly from one shoulder, papers poking out of the half-open top like snaggleteeth.

"Oh my god, hi," she pants when she gets to me. "Is the list up?"

"I don't know," I say. "I just got here."

"Let's go in." She grabs my arm like we've known each other forever, and we run up the steps and through the door together, our kilts flapping against our legs.

Ms. Gutierrez is walking toward the theater doors, a sheet of paper and a roll of tape in her hand, and Lydia squeals at the sight of her. "Hi, girls," she calls. I search her face for clues about whether we made it, but she just smiles. Would she smile even if it were bad news? Does she feel sorry for us because we didn't get in, or is she being mysterious?

"Is that the list?" Lydia breathes.

Ms. Gutierrez laughs. "Give me a second to tape it up." She shoos us back, and we retreat a tiny bit. I try to read the list over her shoulder, but her hair is big and curly, and it totally blocks my view.

Five more girls push through the auditorium doors as Ms. Gutierrez tapes up the sheet, all of them talking over one another. When they see the paper, they scream and rush forward like it's a juicy steak and they're wolves who haven't eaten in a week. Ms. Gutierrez scrambles out of the way, laughing as she heads back toward her office to avoid the chaos.

Lydia and I get to the door first, fingers skimming down the list of names. Neither of us is cast as Cinderella—that role went to Kiara, the girl who sang first at auditions. She totally deserves it, and it's not hard to be happy for her. Neither of us is the fairy godmother or the stepmother, and neither of us is a stepsister—that's kind of disappointing, since I thought I did a great job with Portia. But when we get to the ten names listed under "ensemble," there we both are, one right after the other. My name is at the very top, and I like to think that means I deserve it the most. At the bottom of the page, it says that the first read-through will be in the auditorium on Monday afternoon.

Even as I stare at my name on the list, part of me still can't totally believe this is real. I, Abbi Carrington—the girl who cried at the talent show, the girl who refused to join any activity where she might have to speak to other people—was brave enough to audition for a play and talented enough to be cast in it.

Abby squirms beneath my skin, panic racing through her anxious little heart. I squash her down.

"We did it!" Lydia shrieks. "We're in!" And when she grabs me in a hug, I squeeze her back and jump with her, letting the waterfall of our combined joy shower down on me.

"Oh my god, move over!" shouts one of the girls behind us.

"You're blocking the list!" We step to the side, clinging to each other's arms and stumbling over each other's feet, and the river of girls flows in to fill the space. More shrieks go up as they find their names. One girl who isn't on the list starts to cry and is guided out of the building by her friend.

"We are going to eat *so* many cookies tonight," Lydia gushes. She has a bright spot of pink on each cheek, and her eyes are all lit up.

I nod hard. "We'll put in double chocolate chips."

"*Triple* chocolate chips."

"Why even make the cookies at all? Let's just eat the chocolate chips."

Lydia laughs, and I start to say something else when I spot Sydney in the crowd of girls pushing through the main door. She was so sure I couldn't be in the play, and now she's going to see that I was right all along. Maybe now she'll finally respect me. My parents are always telling me I should try to cut Sydney some slack, that sometimes she has a hard time "directing her feelings appropriately," which means she takes things out on people who don't deserve it. It's not always easy for me to forgive her, but if she apologizes and says she supports me, I can totally do it this time. I'm ready.

"Hang on a second," I say to Lydia.

Syd hasn't noticed me yet; she's focused on the list. I move toward the wall so I'll have a clear view of her when she first sees my name. I can't wait to see the surprise that transforms her face.

People have spotted Sydney now and they shift out of the way like she's a celebrity. A bunch of girls say hi, but Syd just gives a few curt nods and doesn't answer anyone.

"Did Sydney audition for the play?" someone whispers behind me.

"No," someone else says. "We would've seen her."

"Maybe she had a private audition with Ms. Gutierrez?"

"How could she be in the play with all her Committee stuff, though?"

"Well, if she didn't audition, then why is she here?"

"Shh, she'll hear you talking about her!"

Syd has reached the list now, and her eyes skim down the paper. I see the moment she gets to my name, but the expression that crosses her face isn't the one I expected. Her lips part and her eyebrows fly up and her forehead crinkles, and for a moment she looks almost . . . afraid. But that doesn't make any sense.

The look is fleeting, like a cloud passing over the sun. And then my sister's mask of calm indifference falls right back into place, and I wonder if I saw what I think I saw at all.

"Syd," I say quietly, and even though we're in a noisy lobby, she looks straight at me. Our eyes lock for the space of one, two, three heartbeats, and the unreadable expression on her face doesn't change at all.

She shakes her head, the tiniest movement. She reaches up and rubs her left eye under her glasses.

And then, without saying one word to me, she turns around

and pushes through the crowd. No *Congratulations*. No *You were right*. I see a flash of her ponytail as the door slams behind her, and she's gone.

• • •

I try to make myself believe that Syd's attitude doesn't matter. I'm proud of myself, and when I call Mom and Dad to tell them the good news, they're proud of me too. When Christina gets home, I tell her too, and she announces that she made the tennis team, and we throw our arms around each other and jump up and down and scream. It doesn't make the little pebble of hurt in my chest melt away, but it makes it easier to deal with.

I introduce Lydia and Christina that night at dinner. I wonder if Christina will be overwhelmed by Lydia's bouncy enthusiasm, but she seems to like her right away. Lydia tells long, roundabout stories that make Christina laugh, which is good, because it means I can tune out a little bit. My sister is sitting two tables away, right in my sight line, surrounded by a group of popular eighth graders who keep laughing uproariously at her jokes. It's hard to stop picturing that blank, cold look on her face, to stop replaying in my mind the way the door slammed behind her. Everyone treats her like royalty around here; why can't she be happy that I got one thing I want too? Does she think I'm trying to steal her spotlight? Can't she see that I just want my own for a change?

A wave of tiredness washes over me, making my limbs and eyelids feel heavy. Part of me wants to ask Christina and Lydia if we can do cookies tomorrow instead. But I obviously can't back out of my very first hangout with my new friends. I want so badly for them to like me, and if I botch this chance, I have no idea if I'll get another one.

When Lydia hops out of her chair and asks if we're ready to go, I shoot her a bright smile and tell her I am *so* ready.

We find Amelia when we get back to Stronger Hall, and she unlocks the kitchen and helps us find the ingredients we need. As Christina and I mix butter and sugar, spraying chunks of it everywhere with the handheld beaters, Lydia crams a handful of chocolate chips into her mouth, puts on some superfast music, and starts dancing. We crack up as we watch her shake her butt and wave her hands. Little sparks of nervousness swim through my blood at the thought of dancing with her, but I know Abbi is the kind of friend who would abandon the mixing bowl and join in. So I force myself to put down the beaters and shuffle out into the middle of the kitchen, and when Lydia grabs my hand and spins me around, I'm instantly glad I did. Even Christina starts dancing after a minute, bumping my hip with hers, and then we're all laughing, and I don't think I've ever felt as much a part of something as I do right at that moment. I'm so glad I didn't ask for a rain check.

Another girl sticks her head in the door. She's got long black hair, and she's wearing pink pajama pants printed with ice-cream cones. I stop dancing right away; I'm ready for Lydia and Christina to see me acting goofy, but it's different with total strangers.

"Hey," the girl says. I think she's going to ask us to quiet down, but instead she asks, "Which one of you is Abbi?"

"Me," I say, and my heart starts hammering. Am I in trouble or something?

"You're Sydney Carrington's sister, right?"

I nod, and she pulls a pale pink form out of the pocket of her pants. "Do you think you could take this to Petition Day for me tomorrow?"

I wipe my hands on a towel to get rid of the excess sugar and take the form. ROOM RESERVATION REQUEST: *SATOMI YAMAMOTO*, it says across the top. Satomi has written a long explanation about how Robotics Club needs to reserve an entire building because vibrations from people walking around will somehow mess up the data they need to collect. "Don't you have to present this to the Committee yourself?" I ask.

"No, I checked the box for a proxy, see?"

"What's a proxy?" Old Abby never would've asked for an explanation of a word she didn't know, but asking now feels necessary, not embarrassing.

"It's someone who does something in someone else's place," Satomi says.

I hold the form out to her. "Sorry, but I'm not going to Petition Day tomorrow. Can one of your friends take it for you if you can't go?"

"Oh, it's not that I *can't* go," she says. "It's that Sydney doesn't like me. I beat her in a debate in history class last year, and since then she's . . . Well, she's your sister, so I don't want

43

to say anything bad about her, but you know how she is. And people are saying all the other Committee members do whatever she wants, so I doubt she'd approve my petition. But she'll say yes if *you* ask, right?"

I'm still trying to process this when another girl comes in, this one with red glasses and long blond bangs that are falling in her eyes. She's holding a yellow form. "Is this her?" she asks. When Satomi nods, she says, "Hi, I'm Bridget. Art Club really needs new acrylic paints—I heard you can get them for us?"

I didn't tell anyone that my sister is the president of the Committee, but it seems like the news has spread like wildfire anyway. "How do you guys even know Sydney's my sister?" I ask.

"Grace told us," Bridget says just as a third girl arrives, wearing a gigantic purple sweatshirt that almost reaches her knees. In her hand is a matching purple form.

"Are you Abbi?" she asks.

"This is Nadiya," Satomi says. "Can she get in on this too? As long as you're already going to Petition Day for us?"

I haven't actually said I'll go for them, but all three of them are staring at me now, and I can feel Christina and Lydia looking at me from behind; I'm skewered by their gazes like a chunk of meat on a shish kebab. Old Abby would've panicked to have so many people looking at her at once. But Abbi is capable and competent and happy to help people who need it. They're right—it was super easy for me to get my request approved last Petition Day, and I could probably do it again. Today has shown me what it's like to have two new friends, and it's pretty much the best thing ever; what if I could have *five* new friends? Getting these girls what they want will definitely make them like me, and it'll only take me a few minutes.

"So, you'll help us, right?" Bridget asks me.

I put on my brightest Abbi smile, give my braid a confident flip, and hold out my hand to collect their forms. "Of course I'll help," I say. "You can totally count on me."

CHAPTER 6

The basement of the Student Center is even more crowded today than it was on Tuesday—girls swarm around the table of petition forms like a bunch of bees around the last flower on earth. But today I have my paperwork done ahead of time—or Satomi's, Bridget's, and Nadiya's paperwork, I guess—and I'm able to get in line as soon as I arrive. There are only two people ahead of me, so I'll be in the Student Government Office in no time. The three girls—my three new friends?—are grouped on a couch, anxiously awaiting good news. I can't see them from here, but I know they're sending me luck.

I'm not sure if I'm more or less nervous than I was the last time I stood in this line. On the one hand, everything is less scary when you've done it before. On Tuesday, I had no idea what to expect, and now I know exactly what I'll see when I walk into that room. I spent lots of time practicing what I'm going to say when I present the petitions, and there's no reason I won't be able to perform these lines just like I performed Cinderella's and Portia's at my audition. Plus, I'm not asking for anything I personally want, so if my petitions aren't approved, it won't affect me directly.

But on the other hand, there's a lot more at stake now than there was at the last Petition Day. On Tuesday, the worst that could've happened was that I didn't get new blinds. But this time, a few minutes inside that room could change everything for me. People all over the school are clearly talking about me, about how I have an in with the Committee—Nadiya and Bridget are seventh graders who don't even live in my dorm, and they still knew where to find me. If I succeed today, they'll tell their friends, and those people will tell *their* friends, and everyone will start sending me in to petition for them. It hasn't even been a week since I reinvented myself, and I'm already on the brink of becoming the voice of the people. But if I fail, it'll show everyone at Brookside that they were wrong about me, that I'm just another boring sixth grader with nothing special to offer. I might never get another chance to be popular; once people start thinking of you a certain way, it's almost impossible to start over. If I learned anything at my old school, it's that.

I straighten my spine and tell myself there's no *if* I succeed, only *when* I succeed. Everything about me is different here, and this is going to be different too. At Brookside, I'm a winner.

The door opens, and the first girl goes into the office with her form, a blue maintenance request. She emerges a minute later with an APPROVED stamp, and the girl in front of me takes her place. She comes out looking happy too, and she holds the door for me. I lift my chin and walk into the room.

Sydney looks surprised to see me. "Abby," she says, and somehow I can tell she's spelling it wrong in her head, even though she saw the *i* on my last petition form. "Did you not get your blinds?"

"No, the blinds are fine," I say. "They got replaced yesterday. Thank you."

"What can we help you with today?" asks the girl to Syd's left—she's eating cereal again, and her fingertips are dusted with cinnamon and sugar.

I lay my three forms on the table, the corners neatly aligned— yellow, purple, pink. "I'm here as a proxy to present these petitions."

My sister's eyebrows scrunch together, and she's silent for long enough that the girl with the dragon pin says, "Sydney? That's okay, right?"

"I . . . Yeah, I guess," Sydney says. She doesn't seem totally on board, but I guess there's no rule against what I'm doing because she pulls the first form toward her. "Bridget Konditori: petition for three hundred dollars for Art Club to buy acrylic paints."

I know most budget requests don't get approved immediately— the Committee likes to debate them at their morning meetings, when they're alone and have more time to talk them through.

But Bridget is counting on me, and I want to try to get her this money right now. I take a deep breath and launch into the lines I've memorized. "Acrylic paint goes a long way, and you can get a lot for three hundred dollars," I say. "There are a bunch of really fun things you can do with it."

Syd looks surprised, and I realize she's not used to Abbi yet—the sister she knows wouldn't talk any more than necessary. It's weird to think that there are so many people who know my new self better than my family does.

I keep going. "Remember that painting I made last year with the gold and blue swirls, the one that won the prize in the art fair? The one you said looked like a star exploding? That was acrylic." If I want some respect from my sister, reminding her that there are things I'm good at can only help.

"I really hope you approve this one because I'm still thinking about joining Art Club," I continue. "Bridget seems super nice, and it's not that much money, and I think it would—"

"*Okay,*" Syd says like I'm giving her a headache. "All in favor?" She puts up her hand, and all the other girls' hands follow. Maybe she just called a vote because she wanted me to stop talking, but I don't care—I've proven that I can make the people in this room listen to what I have to say. No matter what happens now, I can go back to one of the girls with a win. Bridget will be so grateful to me, and gratitude makes people love you. The success gives me more confidence, and I stand up even straighter, tilting my chin up a little more.

Syd pulls the next paper toward her. "Nadiya Mirza: petition for more hot vegetarian entrées in the dining hall."

"She said she's eaten peanut butter and jelly three nights this week," I say.

"I've eaten grilled cheese three times," says Cereal Girl. "She's right—so much of the hot stuff has meat in it. I guess you can always have the grill make you a veggie burger, but they're honestly not that good."

The girl on her other side giggles, showing the bright pink rubber bands on her braces. "How would you even have room for a veggie burger? Aren't you full from all that cereal?"

"Why do you think I eat all this cereal in the first place? I'm hungry all the time! I'm not getting nearly enough calories to—"

"Okay," Syd says, and both of them shut up. "Gianna, I have no problem with this as long as you take point with the dining hall manager."

Cereal Girl nods. "Sure. I can do that. I'll email her tonight."

"All right. Everyone else in favor?" The other girls say aye, and Syd presses the PENDING stamp down on the paper. I'm two for three now. Even if I can't get the last petition approved, I've still done an impressive job. More people are going to be happy with me than disappointed.

"Satomi Yamamoto: room request for Robotics Club," Syd reads aloud from the third paper. Her nose wrinkles when she says Satomi's name, the way it always used to when I chose something she didn't like for family movie night. This is going to be the hardest one; Satomi specifically said that my sister didn't like her, and I saw proof on Tuesday that Sydney has no problem denying legitimate requests to people she has grudges against.

"She's requesting a completely empty building for three hours for an experiment next week." Syd reads the whole explanation about the vibrations, then replaces the paper on the desk. "We don't usually let people reserve entire *buildings*. We don't have the space for that."

"We're the Committee," says Cereal Girl. "Can't we do whatever we want?"

"Satomi Yamamoto is—" Syd starts, but I don't wait to hear the end of her sentence.

"I think you should approve it," I say. "It's only three hours, and there are probably plenty of empty buildings after classes are out for the day, right?" My sister opens her mouth to speak again, but I don't let her get a word in. "You're obviously not Satomi's biggest fan, but that's all the more reason why you should approve this right now, while you're dealing with me. If I can't get her the space, she'll just come back on Tuesday and ask for it herself. I'm sure you have better things to do than sit here and consider the same petitions over and over." The lines come out smoothly, exactly like I practiced.

All three of the other Committee members glance at each other and nod silently, but Sydney just sits there, eyeing the DENIED stamp. I'm going to have to push harder.

"It's probably difficult for you to give her what she wants after she beat you in that debate last year," I say, making my voice sympathetic. "I know how much you hate losing, and—"

"It has nothing to do with that," Syd snaps. "I want to make sure that—ugh, whatever. I don't even care. All in favor?" She's doing the eye-rubbing thing again, and I can see I've shaken her confidence. Good—now she knows how I felt when she said there was no way I could handle being in the play.

The other girls look at my sister, obviously confused about what they're supposed to do, until Sydney raises her hand. Her other hand is clenched into a fist, but I'm pretty sure I'm the only one who notices. "Aye," she says.

"Aye," the other girls echo.

"The motion passes." Syd slams her APPROVED stamp down on the paper so hard the ink smears. "We'll contact Satomi directly when we find a building Robotics Club can use."

Even though my sister does *not* look happy, my heart leaps. I did it. It's the same feeling I had up onstage the other day, slipping seamlessly into the skin of the evil stepsister and letting her speak with my voice. I'm *good* at this. I'm a convincing person.

Maybe I could've beaten Syd in that debate in history class last year too.

• • •

I'm getting ready for bed, basking in my win and remembering the crowd of girls that swarmed around me at dinner, asking me to advocate for them, when my phone chimes. I grab it off my bed to find a text from my sister.

You know you don't have to petition for other people just because they ask you to, right?

I want to, I reply.

The "someone's typing" dots pop up, then disappear, then pop up again, then disappear again. It makes me smile; my sister is clearly struggling to think of a reason why I should stop acting as a proxy, but she's having trouble finding a convincing one. It's not like she can come right out and say, *I hate that you did such a good job of presenting your case that you made me approve petitions I wanted to reject.*

Finally another message pops up on the screen: *It's not going to make them be friends with you, you know. They don't want to hang out with you. They're just using you because you're my sister.*

Rage floods through me. I am so sick of Sydney trying to cut me down and make me feel like nothing good can ever happen to me. I'm sick of her wanting to be the only one who's successful, the only one who has managed to surround herself with new friends. The people I petitioned for today *do* like me; Bridget invited me to sit with her at dinner, and she even brought me frozen yogurt with Cocoa Krispies on top when she got some for herself. (Totally genius, by the way.) You don't randomly bring someone dessert if you don't want to be friends with her.

Why can't Sydney accept that things are finally going *well* for me?

I pick up my pillow and throw it across the room, then immediately feel ridiculous and pick it up before Christina returns from the shower. I force myself to take a few deep breaths before I text Sydney back. One of us has to be the mature sister, and clearly it's going to have to be me.

You can think whatever you want, but you can't control what I do.

I wait for a response, but it never comes. Instead, five

minutes later, a campus-wide email appears in my inbox. It's from the Committee, stating that each student can only present one petition per Petition Day. Of course Sydney would find another way to have the last word, to remind me that she has more power than I do.

I wait for my anger to flare up again, but this time it doesn't come. Honestly it's kind of amazing to know that the most powerful student at Brookside has made a new school-wide policy specifically because of me. At King Elementary, I'm pretty sure nobody would've noticed if I'd evaporated into the air and disappeared. Here I'm already influencing things in a major way, and it's only been six days.

If Sydney wants to play this game, fine. It only makes me want to work harder to prove that I'm a worthy opponent. I sit down at my computer, make a proxy sign-up sheet for the next month, print it out, and post it on my door.

By the next evening, the sheet is completely full. Looking at it makes me tired, but I refuse to let myself think about that. Being an important, influential person on campus takes effort, and I'm more than up to the task.

Abbi Carrington, voice of the people. It has a nice ring to it.

CHAPTER 7

Abby

I don't think I've ever been desperate for a weekend to be over before, but our first play rehearsal is on Monday, and it can't come soon enough. We're going to do a full read-through of the play, which means I'll get to find out which ensemble lines are mine, and when we get to the songs, those of us who know them will sing while Ms. Solomon plays the piano so everyone can get familiar with the music. I know every word of every song already—I downloaded the original cast album and listened to it over and over as soon as I decided to audition—and I know Lydia and Grace do too. I can't wait to sing with them and the rest of my cast, our voices blending and mixing until you can't tell one from another.

The moment the last bell rings, I head across the quad to the auditorium; my feet feel so light and floaty that it's hard to keep myself from skipping. Grace and Kiara and a few other girls are already clustered outside the door when I arrive, and I jog up the steps to meet them. "Hi," I chirp in my friendliest Abbi voice.

Grace turns around and says hello, but she has a weird look on her face, and then I notice the handwritten sign taped to the auditorium door: THIS BUILDING IS OFF-LIMITS. DO NOT ENTER. There's a strip of caution tape looped through the handles of the double doors, tying them together.

"I texted Ms. Gutierrez and Ms. Solomon," Grace says. "They'll be here in a minute."

"What do you think happened?" one of the girls asks. "Do you think the theater's flooded or something?"

"I totally want to see that," says another girl.

"Maybe there's a gas leak."

"Or maybe there are *bees* inside. Like, tons and tons of *bees*."

"Hi, girls!" says a voice behind us, and Grace's face relaxes as Ms. Gutierrez strides purposefully up the stairs. Our director frowns as she looks at the sign and the caution tape. "It's weird that I didn't get an email about the building being off-limits—my office is in there." She tries to pull the doors open enough to peer inside, and we all stand on our toes to look, but the caution tape is tied too tightly, and it holds the handles shut. "Hang on, I'm going to make a quick call," she says.

She pulls out her phone and dials what I assume is the administration office, and we all go quiet so she can hear. But nobody answers, and she sighs and hangs up. "Well, I can't get your scripts for the read-through if we're not allowed inside.

I've got one in my bag, but there's no way twenty of us can share."

"Hey," Ms. Solomon says as she joins us. "The auditorium's closed?"

"Apparently," Ms. Gutierrez says. "I tried calling Cynthia, but nobody picked up."

"I have my score," Ms. Solomon says. "Is there another piano somewhere that we can use? At least we can do a sing-through."

"The choir room?" Kiara suggests.

Ms. Solomon shakes her head. "Today's the first choir rehearsal. And the jazz ensemble is in the band room."

"There are a few pianos in the practice rooms in the basement of Rose, but you can barely fit two people in one of those," says Grace.

"I think there's a piano in the common room of Kaufman," says a girl I don't know. "Do you want me to go over and check?"

"Thanks, Riley, that would be really helpful," says Ms. Gutierrez, and the girl runs off.

The rest of the cast arrives in twos and threes as the teachers try to figure out what to do, and after a few minutes, Lydia slips in beside me. When I explain what's happening, her face falls. "Man, I was really looking forward to this."

"I know, me too," I say.

Riley comes running back, breathing hard. "The piano in Kaufman is being tuned," she says. "I asked the guy if he could come back later, but he said he drove an hour to get here and that this was his only available slot."

Ms. Gutierrez shakes her head. "This rehearsal is cursed," she says. "Did one of you say the name of the Scottish play in the theater during auditions?"

"What's the Scottish play?" asks someone.

"It's an old theater superstition," Ms. Gutierrez explains. "You aren't allowed to say the word 'Macbeth' inside a theater or it's bad luck for the production. If you accidentally say it, you have to go outside, turn around three times, spit, swear, knock on the door, and ask to be let back in." Kiara nods like she's familiar with this procedure.

"Whoa," says the girl. "Have you ever had to do that?"

"Of course," says Ms. Gutierrez. "Anyone who works in theater has. Anyway, here's what we're going to do. We can't very well have a read-through with no room, no piano, and no scripts. But it's a beautiful day, so let's find some space on the quad, and we can play theater games and get to know each other. We'll reschedule the read-through for Wednesday. We have the theater booked that day, right, Grace?"

Grace nods. "It's all taken care of."

I raise my hand. "I have the cast album on my phone, if we want to sing through some of it after we play games," I suggest.

Ms. Gutierrez smiles at me and says, "Thank you, Abbi, that's a great idea," and it makes a bloom of warmth unfurl in the center of my chest.

We follow our director across the quad like twenty baby ducks. It *is* a gorgeous day, warm and hazy, and the stripes of sun between the buildings make the grass glow a bright emerald green. We find a spot under a giant tree, its branches reaching out like it wants to protect us, and Ms. Gutierrez tells us to form a circle. We go around and say our names, what part we're going to play, and what we would wish for if we had a fairy godmother. I used to get so nervous to speak in front of groups even when it was just for a few seconds like this—my guts would twist like snarled yarn until it was my turn, and my fingertips would tingle with adrenaline for minutes afterward. But this time, to my surprise and relief, I'm able to breathe and stay calm. When it's my turn, I want to say that I'd wish to always feel this connected to a group, this much a part of something bigger than myself. But that seems too personal, so I say I'd wish for a teleporter.

Ms. Solomon leads us through a series of vocal warm-ups, contorting our faces and repeating silly tongue twisters about yellow leather and knapsacks and unique New York. We all look incredibly goofy, and some of the girls passing on the paths stare at us. But because we're all doing it together, it doesn't feel embarrassing, even when people laugh. Ms. Gutierrez teaches us a game called Zip Zap Zop, which tests your speed and concentration, and I focus so hard that I forget to be nervous. Then we pair off and take turns sculpting our partners into living statues, and I laugh so hard I almost fall down when Lydia makes me stand on one foot like a flamingo, one hand planted on my butt and the other sticking a finger in my ear. It turns out drama games are really fun.

And then Ms. Gutierrez says it's time to play Freeze.

"Two people will start a scene," she explains. "At any point, another person can yell 'Freeze!' and both people freeze exactly as they are. The new person takes the place of one of the actors, assumes her position, and starts another completely unrelated scene. A few of you already know how to play—Grace and Kiara, you want to start?"

"Sure," says Grace, and they hop up and take their place at the front of the group.

Without even taking a minute to think, Kiara says, "Doctor, I'm so glad you could see me on such short notice. I have a serious problem."

Grace pretends to write on a clipboard. "What seems to be the issue?"

Kiara holds up her arm. "Well, as you can see, my arm has turned into an octopus tentacle."

Everyone laughs, but Grace and Kiara manage to keep straight faces. "So it has," Grace says, turning the arm over and looking at it from different angles. "Fascinating. Well, the good news is that it's a lovely shade of blue, and those suckers look extremely healthy."

"Yes, it's a good tentacle, as tentacles go," Kiara agrees. "I'm not having any issues using it. The problem is that it keeps trying to strangle random people on the street. I don't have any control over what it—" She twitches. "Oh no. It's doing it again! Help!" She makes a comically horrified face as she snakes her arm around Grace's neck, and everyone cracks up. I'm completely in awe of the two of them and also completely sure that I cannot do what they're doing. How are they thinking so fast and managing to be funny at the same time?

"Freeze!" shouts a girl named Salima. She tags out Kiara,

who's now lying on the ground, and bellows, "This is it, Harold! The baby's coming!"

While everyone's screaming with laughter, I lean over to Lydia and whisper, "How are they doing this?"

"I don't know," she says. "It's so quick. But I guess that's the point? I guess you just . . . say whatever comes into your head?"

But I can't say whatever comes into my head. Everything I say and do these days is carefully calculated and practiced. I've gotten really good at being Abbi, but it still takes effort, even when I'm having a normal conversation with one person. I'm not ready for an unplanned performance yet.

A girl named Kendall tags in and starts a scene about a pizza chef, and then Riley starts a scene about flying a plane, and then Kiara hops back in with a scene about a ghost possessing her computer.

"Let's let some of the newcomers have a turn," Ms. Gutierrez says, and she looks over at us.

I feel Lydia take a deep breath beside me, and as Kiara raises her hand high above her head, Lydia yells, "Freeze!" and hops to her feet. Lydia tags Kiara out, then says in a voice like a very small child, "Mommy, I can't reach the Frosted Flakes!"

I'm so impressed with how my friend throws herself into the game even when she doesn't really know what she's doing—she doesn't get tagged out for a while, and she successfully plays a shoe salesperson, a granny, and a movie star on the red carpet. When she finally sits down next to me again, she's flushed and breathing hard, but she whispers, "It wasn't that hard! It was fun!"

I nod and tell her she did great, and then I sit there tense as a bowstring, hands balled into fists in my lap, waiting for an opening. The scenes turn over and over, flip-book quick, but I can't find a gap I think I can fill.

Finally Ms. Gutierrez says, "Has everyone had a turn?" She looks around the circle, and for the first moment since I got to Brookside, I try to banish Abbi from my body and fade into the background so her eyes will skate right past me. But some traces of my new self must still be there, because she says, "Abbi and Sasha—you haven't been in yet, right? Go ahead and take one turn each."

A new scene starts and Sasha calls freeze almost immediately, then starts a scene about a waiter who drops an enormous pile of dishes. I will my voice to cooperate, for my hand to shoot into the air, but the scene goes on and on, and I just can't do it. Finally Ms. Gutierrez catches my eye and nods, and I know she's not going to let me out of this, so I force my mouth to form the word "Freeze." It comes out quiet, but Sasha and her scene partner Nevaeh stop, and I slowly get to my feet and brush the grass off my skirt. Lydia touches the back of my calf, but it doesn't make me feel better. It makes me wonder if she's noticed the way my legs are trembling.

Sasha has one hand over her head like she's swimming the backstroke, so I tag her out. For a second it's like every word in the English language has fled my brain, leaving a terrifying void behind. I find myself twisting the end of my braid around my finger, and I force myself to stop. "Um," I say, and forty expectant eyes look up at me. They all saw me sing at the audition, confident and sure, and they must be wondering what's wrong with me now. It's too similar to how I used to feel standing in front of a class, and for a second I'm sure my knees are going to buckle.

Boooo-hooooo, goes the ghost of Evan Hamilton inside my head.

That's not going to happen today, responds a stern Abbi voice. *Say something. Literally anything is fine.*

"Help, I'm drowning!" I yell, and I can feel the entire group release a collective breath.

Nevaeh rushes to my side, making motions like she's treading water. "Here, grab on to this life raft!"

"No, it's leaking air!" I say. "It has a hole in it from . . . um . . ." From what? I desperately scrabble around in my brain for an idea, but I feel like I'm having an out-of-body experience, like I have no control over what words are going to come out of my mouth. Finally I hear myself say, ". . . from where a shark bit it!"

Nevaeh loops my arm around her shoulders. "Hang on to me, then. Did the shark bite you? Is that why you can't swim?"

"No," I say. "Not yet. But it could happen any second."

"Do you see any sharks now?"

I pretend to scan the horizon. "No, do you?"

She points. "There's one! Grab it! We can hang on to its back and ride it to safety!"

"But—"

"Annnnd scene!" says Ms. Gutierrez, clapping for punctuation. My whole body relaxes—it's over—and I sag against Nevaeh. She staggers a little, surprised to have to hold me up for real.

"That was great, girls," our director says. "One tip for the future, though—improv games like this work best when we say 'Yes, and . . .' instead of 'No.' For example, in that last round, Nevaeh provided several ideas—a life raft, a shark bite—but Abbi chose not to move the scene in those directions. Next time, Abbi, try to accept what your scene partner gives you and take it one step further—like, you might say yes, the shark bit off your entire leg and you have to dive down and catch it before it sinks to the bottom. Does that make sense?"

She says it in the nicest possible way, but it still stings like the snap of a rubber band. It doesn't seem like the other girls are judging me, but I can feel my face turning bubble-gum pink anyway. It's my very first day of rehearsal, and I've already been singled out as a failure.

Ms. Gutierrez touches my shoulder gently. "I'm not putting you on the spot," she says. "That was just the most recent example, since you went last. Okay?"

I nod, but I don't say anything. If I open my mouth, I'm afraid I might cry.

"All right, wonderful," Ms. Gutierrez says. "Should we move along to our sing-through? Abbi, you said you have the cast album on your phone, right?"

I nod again, and this time I instantly start to feel better. Maybe I'm not good at making things up on the spot, even in my Abbi form, but I know I can sing these songs—I've been practicing. I pull up the album, click play on "The Prince Is Giving a Ball," and put my phone on the grass, and everyone else forms a tight circle around it. And when the music starts,

I'm the first one to start singing, and Ms. Gutierrez smiles at me as she joins in. She has a beautiful voice, as good as the people on the recording.

Even without an auditorium or a piano, singing with her and the rest of my cast is as perfect as I'd hoped it would be.

As we move into "In My Own Little Corner," I tell myself not to worry—I might never need to improvise again. Once we get our scripts, we'll be learning our blocking and our music at rehearsal, not playing games. I'll never be asked to improvise a class presentation, and I can always practice what I'm going to say before I present a petition for myself or someone else.

I may have found the one thing Abbi can't do, but I'm still going to be absolutely fine.

CHAPTER 8

On Wednesday morning, the day of our makeup read-through, I wake to someone banging on our door. Christina turns over and pulls a pillow over her face, and I consider doing the same—I have ten more minutes before my alarm is supposed to go off. I thought staying in character all day every day would get less exhausting, but so far it hasn't, and I need all the sleep I can get. But the knocking gets faster, more frantic sounding, and then someone calls, "Abbi?"

"Just a second," I say, and my voice comes out early-morning croaky. I throw off the covers, stand up, and take a second to let Abbi climb back into my body—no matter how hard I try to hang on to her, she always slips right out of my skin while I'm sleeping. Once I feel settled, I redo my ponytail and pull the door open.

It's Grace, and she looks like a complete wreck; her hair is sticking up on one side, her eyes are red and wet, and she's wearing a bathrobe over her pajamas, the belt trailing on the ground. She has two different socks on, one with hearts and one with giraffes. Before I can ask what's wrong, she says, "Did you check your email?"

"No," I say. "I was asleep. What happened?"

"Ms. Gutierrez quit," Grace says, and two more tears spill down her cheeks.

"She quit the play? Why?" I picture our director leaping around the lawn two days ago, her eyes bright with excitement.

"She quit *Brookside*." Grace wipes her eyes on the cuff of her robe. "She's been my drama teacher since sixth grade, and I was *finally* going to get to be her assistant director after two years of waiting, and now she's just *gone*."

I hear Christina roll over, and I step out into the hall and close the door so I won't bother her. "Did she say why?"

"She got a part in a Broadway show. I guess she went down to New York City and auditioned last weekend. She said it was a last-minute decision, but she feels like this is 'the right career move for her' or whatever. She's leaving tomorrow, so we won't even get to see her again before she goes."

"Wow," I say. "A Broadway show? That's amazing for her."

Grace glares. "Yeah, but not amazing for *us*. She obviously doesn't care about us at all or she wouldn't have auditioned."

"I guess," I say, even though I'm pretty sure I would've quit too if I were her. "Who's going to be our director? Ms. Solomon?"

"I don't think so. I don't think she knows anything about acting or directing."

A cold feeling rears its head in the pit of my stomach and reaches its fingers up my throat, twisting around the question I'm about to ask. "Is there . . . The play is still *happening*, right?" I can't bear the thought that I've finally psyched myself up to act in front of other people and now the opportunity might be ripped away before we've even had a single real rehearsal.

"I don't know," Grace says. "I'm sure they'll try to hire someone new, but with the auditorium being closed mysteriously and all the pianos in the school being off-limits at once and now this . . . Maybe Ms. Gutierrez was right. Maybe someone talked about the Scottish play and now we're cursed."

We *have* had ridiculously bad luck. It could be a curse, or maybe it's a series of coincidences. But when I think about Sydney telling me not to audition for the play, and about that weird expression on her face when she saw the cast list, I suddenly start to think there might be a more straightforward explanation. It seems impossible that my sister could've gotten Ms. Gutierrez a new job, but I still have this gut-deep feeling that she's to blame for everything else that's gone wrong. And if she's the one standing in our way instead of some Scottish theater ghost, maybe I can fix it. I'm probably the *only* one who can.

"We should get ready for class," I tell Grace. "I'll see what I can find out, and we'll talk about it more later, okay?"

"Yeah," she says. She wipes her eyes again, and then she

reaches out and hugs me, quick and unexpected. Nobody has ever come to me for comfort before, and I'm not really sure what to do. I put one arm around her shoulders and sort of awkwardly pat her hair with the other hand, and I guess that's close enough to right, because I feel Grace relax a little. When she pulls away, she looks calmer.

"We'll figure this out," I say with all the Abbi confidence I can muster. "I have some ideas already." I've done a lot to fix things for my classmates this week, and there's no reason I can't do this too. I touch the sign-up sheet on my door and remind myself that I'm the voice of the people now.

Christina's alarm goes off as soon as I come back into the room, and she gives me a halfhearted wave and stumbles off to the bathroom. I should really take a shower—my hair is getting greasy—but instead I pull out my phone and call Sydney, ready to lay into her the moment she picks up. She doesn't answer, so I call again, then again. The third time, it goes straight to voicemail, and I know she's hitting the ignore button, which turns the ice in my stomach into bubbling rage.

PICK UP, I text her, but she doesn't reply.

I throw on my clothes, weave my slightly disgusting hair into a quick side-braid, and storm out the door.

I've never been to my sister's dorm, and even once I pull up a campus map on my phone, it takes me a while to find it—all the ivy-covered brick buildings look the same. I have no idea what room she's in, so I wait in the lobby until a girl in running clothes finally directs me to room 309. When I knock, the lock clicks open almost immediately, and I steel myself to confront my sister. But it's a girl I've never seen before, dressed in a field hockey jersey. Her hair is in two perfect French braids.

"Yeah?" she asks.

"Is this Sydney's room?"

"Yeah."

"Is she here?"

"Nope." The girl squats down and starts messing with something inside a duffel bag.

"Do you know where she went?"

"No idea." A door that I thought was a closet swings open, and another girl comes out—there's a second bedroom on the other side. I guess my sister lives with two friends. The other girl is wearing an identical jersey, track pants, and braids. "Do you know where Sydney went?" the first girl asks.

"Nope," says the second girl. She grabs a matching duffel. "Ready to go?"

"Hang on," I say. "How long ago did she leave? Is she usually gone this early?"

The girls shrug in unison. I don't see how they could possibly not know—they *live* with Sydney—but I just say, "Can I leave a message for her?"

"You can write something on the whiteboard," the first girl says. "I don't know when she'll see it, though. You should probably text her."

"We have to go to practice," says the second girl. "Could you, like . . . move?"

I scoot out of the way, and they lock their door and head off down the hall. One of the duffel bags bangs into my shoulder as they pass, but they don't apologize. I didn't think it was possible, but it looks like my sister actually managed to find roommates as rude as she is.

I scrawl "S—CALL ME—A" on the whiteboard, but there's no way I'm waiting till she returns to get to the bottom of this. I head to the dining hall, more determined than ever, but of course Sydney isn't there. I only have time to grab a bagel before I have to go to class.

The minute the bell rings for lunch, I'm back in the dining hall looking for my sister—she has to eat *sometime*. But girl after girl walks past me, and none of them is her. A few girls from the play wave at me from the table by the juice dispenser and beckon me to come sit with them, and Nadiya and Bridget do the same from a few tables away. I let myself feel a moment of pride that I've already woven myself right into the fabric of Brookside after such a short time. But I'm on a mission. I wave back and keep moving.

I'm walking up and down the aisles between the tables and trying to work out a plan when I spot the Committee member who always wears a dragon pin on her blazer. She's reading, and she's so riveted by her book that she keeps bringing half her sandwich up to her mouth, then putting it down again without actually taking a bite. I approach her and say, "You're Lily, right?" I had looked up the names of the Committee members on Brookside's website, and I'm pretty sure I have them straight.

The girl starts, and it takes her a second to focus on me, like she's coming back from somewhere very far away. I totally get it; I feel the same way when someone interrupts me while I'm reading. "Yeah," she says. And then her eyes widen like she's just registered who I am, and she starts packing up her stuff at top speed, cramming her book into her backpack with one hand while she shoves her sandwich into her mouth with the other.

"Wait," I say. "Can I talk to you for a second?"

She shakes her head hard. "I have to go," she says, even though it's still the beginning of lunch and she was sitting there calmly until I arrived.

"It'll be quick." I sit down next to her, thinking she'll feel more comfortable if I'm not looming over her. But she leaps up like her chair has given her an electric shock, then looks over her shoulder like she's checking to make sure nobody has seen us together.

"I'm not supposed to be talking to you," she says. "If she sees, I could get in—I have to go." And then she's out of the cafeteria so fast I'm surprised a cartoon dust cloud doesn't appear behind her.

There's only one person Lily could be referring to, and it proves that I'm on the right track. Sydney wouldn't have told the Committee they couldn't speak to me unless they had something to hide.

Fortunately I spot Gianna walking into the dining hall with a friend, and I dodge in front of them before they can make it to a table. "Hi," I say, and the smile falls right off her face.

She looks over her shoulder the same way Lily did, and then she says, "Umm. I can't . . . I have to—"

I cut her off. "I know, you're not supposed to talk to me, right? But I really need to ask you some stuff. Can we go somewhere nobody can see us?" She fiddles with the cuff of her blazer, and I can tell she's thinking about saying no, so I continue, "Look, I'm going to keep following you around until you talk to me, so you might as well get it over with."

"Fine," Gianna says. "I'll meet you in the far-right bathroom in three minutes. You go first."

I nod, and as I walk away, I hear Gianna say to her friend, "Don't tell *anyone* I was talking to her."

"Who even is that?" asks her friend.

There's a row of one-person bathrooms right outside the dining hall, and I slip into the one on the right and lock the door, then pace around the little space, twisting my braid around my finger. Gianna clearly doesn't want to give me the information I need, and I have no idea how I'm supposed to force it out of her; I've never done anything like this before. But after a minute, I make myself be still—nervous pacing and braid twirling are Abby things to do, and I need to embody Abbi now more than ever. If the Petition Days I've been to are anything to go by, Abbi's great at getting people to give her the things she wants. There's no reason information should be harder to get than three hundred dollars for Art Club.

I shake out my hair and redo my braid, and by the time I'm done, I feel more like my new self, confident and ready.

A minute later, there's a rap at the door. I open it, and Gianna slips inside and turns the lock behind her. "I only have a minute."

"Then I'll get right to it," I say, and I'm happy with how forceful the words come out. "Is my sister trying to sabotage the play?"

At first Gianna's poker face is pretty good, but then her eyes shift to the side for a second. "What do you mean?"

"I guess I don't have concrete proof," I say. "I just know she didn't want me to audition for some reason, and she seemed annoyed when I got in, and now everything is going wrong for us. And I know she has a lot of power to make things happen, and . . . I don't know, it seems like maybe some of this stuff isn't coincidental."

Gianna seems to relax—I guess it's clear to her how little I know. I shouldn't have been so honest. "I don't really understand what you're asking," she says.

I sigh. "Okay, fine. Did the Committee vote to have the piano in the common room of Kaufman tuned?"

Gianna looks surprised. "Well, yeah. How is that sabotage? How does that even have anything to do with the play?"

This line of questioning clearly isn't going to get me anywhere, so I switch to something else. "Do you know why the auditorium was off-limits on Monday?"

"I'm pretty sure Robotics Club was in there," Gianna says. She takes a tablet out of her bag and opens some sort of calendar app. "Yeah, they were. Aren't you the one who petitioned for that? When they said they needed a whole building nobody else was using? Sydney said the auditorium was free that day, so we gave it to them."

I *know* Grace had reserved the auditorium for that day, and I'm sure Sydney knew it too. Now I'm finally getting somewhere.

"You know Ms. Gutierrez quit, right?" I ask.

Gianna nods. "I heard she's going to be in a Broadway show?"

"Did you talk about what's going to happen with the play at the Committee meeting this morning?"

She sighs and drops her gaze to the floor. "Mm-hmm," she says quietly.

"When is the principal going to start looking for a new director?"

Gianna's eyeing the lock on the door now like she thinks she might be able to slip out of the bathroom without me noticing. "I can't . . . She said I couldn't . . . I'm not supposed to tell you—"

I take a step toward her. "You guys are going to have to tell the cast what's happening before our next rehearsal anyway. I'm going to find out. What does it matter if you tell me now?" Gianna's silent, and I say, "They *are* hiring a new director, right?"

"I don't know," she says, and then her voice drops so low I can barely hear it. "Probably not."

That cold feeling from this morning creeps into my stomach again. "You guys are *canceling* the play?" She doesn't say anything, and I step closer, forcing her to look at me. "Gianna. Tell me what's going on."

It feels incredibly weird to bully her like this, and a big part of me is convinced she's going to see past my tough Abbi exterior and laugh right in my face. But she just shrinks away and mumbles, "Yeah. It's not happening."

"You already voted on it?" Gianna nods. "But why? Can't we get someone else to direct it?"

"There's not enough money in the budget to hire an outside director," she says. "The play was already really expensive. It takes up way more than its fair share of money." It sounds like she's reciting something she's been forced to memorize.

"But why would it have to be an outside director? Isn't the school hiring a new drama teacher? It would be part of their job. It wouldn't cost anything extra."

"I don't know. Anyway, it's too late now. We already voted."

"But Grace and I could appeal that decision on Friday, couldn't we?"

"I guess, but Sydney's going to say no." She swallows hard. "I'm really sorry."

My palms are starting to sting, and I realize I'm digging my nails into them. I force myself to uncurl my fingers. There's a reservoir of words pooling in my chest, all kinds of things I'd like to yell about how ridiculously unfair all of this is, how my sister has no right to take away something I love because of her own petty jealousy. I know it's not about the money; it's about getting back at me, personally. But I also know that even as Abbi, I wouldn't be able to yell at another person—thoughts like this always get caught in my throat when I try to get them out, stopping my breath and reddening my face and leaving me in silent, frustrated tears. I refuse to let that happen now. That kind of thing doesn't happen to the new me.

I take a slow, deep breath, and then I say, "Do *you* think the play should be canceled?"

"No," Gianna says right away. "I love Rodgers and Hammerstein's *Cinderella*. I watched that movie a million times when I was little. I was super looking forward to—"

I cut her off. "So Lily and Maya want it to be canceled?"

"I don't think so." Gianna looks miserable, and I almost feel sorry for her. "They, um . . . Lily said some of the same stuff you are saying in the meeting."

"I don't understand how this happened," I say. "If Sydney's the only one who wants to cancel it, why can't you vote her down? There are three of you and one of her."

Gianna shakes her head hard. She's edged so far toward the door now that her back is pressed against it, her palms flat against the wood on either side of her. "We can't . . . We have to do what she—"

Someone knocks on the door, and relief washes over Gianna's face. "We should get out of here," she says. "Someone needs the bathroom."

"They can use one of the other ones. Just wait a second." My voice comes out like I'm begging, but I can't help it; I know this is my last chance to talk to Gianna. There's no way she's going to let herself get trapped with me again. "I don't understand why you have to do what Sydney says. I know she can be mean, but it's not like she can kick you off the Committee. If you and Lily and Maya think what she's doing is wrong, you can band together and overrule her."

Gianna unlocks the door and shoves her way out into a hallway teeming with girls, but she pauses for a second before the door closes behind her. Her eyes are deep wells of fear.

"No," she says over her shoulder. "That's the thing. We really, *really* can't."

CHAPTER 9

An email goes out to the cast of *Cinderella* first thing the next morning. "Due to Ms. Gutierrez's unexpected departure and the lack of adequate funds to hire an outside director, Brookside regrets to inform you that the fall play is canceled. We will reassess the situation in the spring." There is no mention of hiring a new drama teacher, no further explanation at all. The email is signed by the Committee, but it's obviously from my sister.

It seems weird that there's nothing from the administration. It makes me wonder if Principal Winslow and Vice Principal Rosenberg even know about what's happening.

Next in my inbox is a whole thread of weepy messages from the cast. My phone chimes constantly with texts from Grace, imploring me to come with her to Petition Day tomorrow and beg the Committee to reinstate the play.

This would all be too much for the Old Abby. That part of me still wants to hide under the covers and mourn the fact that the play is gone. Old Abby wants to tell Christina I'm sick, ask her to bring me soup and hot chocolate and listen to me as I wallow in my sorrow.

But Abbi knows hot chocolate and tears aren't going to fix anything. My sister is trying to bring us down, and I'm the only one who can fight her, so I have to do everything in my power to try.

I respond to the cast email chain. *Don't lose hope yet. My sister is the president of the Committee, and I'm pretty good at getting her to do what I want. I might be able to fix this.* I tell Grace that we should wait until next week to petition the Committee together because I want to talk to Sydney alone first. I get back a bunch of grateful, encouraging messages from the cast saying they know I can convince the Committee, and it boosts my confidence. People are counting on me, and I can totally do this.

I spend every moment that I'm not in class on Thursday searching for Sydney. I try the library, the Student Government Office before first period, her room before and after dinner, the infirmary, the quad, even the chapel. But she must have spies reporting my movements back to her, because I never manage to catch so much as a glimpse of her, and she doesn't respond to any of my texts. She's had an entire year to learn every nook and cranny and secret passageway of this school, and I haven't even been here two weeks. I feel like a detective who's been tasked with tracking down a master criminal her first day on the job.

But I know one place my sister will be for sure. She may be working hard to avoid me, but she'd never skip a Petition Day.

• • •

I stand in line after class on Friday, my heart skipping along at a faster pace than usual. Sydney stares me down from the moment I enter the room with my proxy petition, and it's hard not to launch into the argument I want to have right away. But I know she won't reveal anything if I grill her in front of the other Committee members, so I force myself to be patient. I present my petition, and she can't think of a good reason to deny it—it's for a girl named Preeti, who needs a week-long exemption from PE because of a sprained toe. Sydney seems relieved as I turn to go, and I smile to myself. She has no idea how soon she'll be seeing me again.

I pick a spot on an old plaid couch and wait for all the other petitioners to take their turns. It's boring, but I don't allow myself to look at my homework or my phone—Syd is wily enough that I'm afraid she might slip through my fingers if I look down for even a moment. Instead I read every piece of paper on the giant bulletin board across from me: reminders about club activities and movie nights and the fall dance with our brother school. There are campaign posters too—elections for sixth-grade representatives are in a few weeks, and it looks like three people are running. The best poster has a really good drawing of a girl in a superhero outfit, flying through the air as her twists and her cape stream out behind her. SAVE THE DAY AND VOTE FOR ANGELINA, it says.

After what seems like forever, all the petitioners finally clear out, and I hear a burst of laughter as the Student Government Office door opens one last time. I get set to jump up, but it's just Gianna, Lily, and Maya; Sydney isn't with them. Gianna spots me and immediately looks away, hustling her friends toward the stairs and out the door.

I hoist myself off the couch—it has some broken springs, and I've sunken in deeper than I expected—and pad down the hall to the office. The door is closed most of the way, but it's not latched, so I push it open without knocking. My sister is sitting at the table, sorting through a stack of petition forms. "Petition Day is over," she says without even looking up. "If you want something, you'll have to come back on Tuesday."

"I'm not here to petition," I say. "I just need to talk to you."

Sydney freezes, and when she finally looks up, she does *not* look happy to see me. "This isn't a good time," she says in a flat, expressionless voice.

I move into the room anyway, pull the door shut behind me, and stand directly across the table from her. She's wearing those giant lace-up boots again, but I try not to let them intimidate me. "It seems like there's never a good time. I've been trying to get hold of you since Wednesday morning. I can never find you anywhere, and you don't return my texts or my phone calls. I've left you a million messages."

She shrugs and looks back down at her pile of papers. "I'm busy. I'm the president, in case you haven't noticed."

"Yeah, I'm busy too. But this is important. Give me ten minutes, and then I'll leave you alone, okay?"

My sister rolls her eyes like I'm asking her to shovel a mile-long driveway in the middle of an ice storm. "Fine," she finally says. "What can I help you with?"

I sigh, already frustrated. "Come on, Syd. You can drop the act. I know the rest of the Committee thinks you're all scary and important for some reason, but I'm your sister. There's nobody else here. Just talk to me like normal, okay?"

"I don't know what you mean," Sydney says in that same flat voice. "This is how I talk."

"It's not how you used to talk."

"Well, things change." She crosses her arms tight over her chest. "Do you have something you actually want to say? Or are you here to criticize how I speak?"

I'm obviously not going to find a softer version of Sydney hiding inside this one, so I'm going to have to work with what she's giving me. "Fine," I say. "You canceled the play."

"*I* didn't do anything," Sydney says. "It wasn't feasible to do the play this fall, so the Committee voted unanimously to hold off until the spring."

I know from talking to Gianna that it was only unanimous because Syd somehow forced it to be, but I haven't figured out how yet, so I can't call her out on it. "It was important to a lot of people," I say. "It was important to *me*."

"I'm sorry you're upset," she says, and it comes out like she's talking to a five-year-old. "But there can't be a play without a director, and there isn't enough money to hire another one now that Ms. Gutierrez has quit."

"Ms. Gutierrez was a *teacher*," I argue. "Won't they just replace her? People take drama as a class. Whoever they hire can take over."

"It takes a long time to hire new faculty," Sydney says. "It'll probably be too late by the time they find someone."

"But the whole cast—"

Syd talks right over me. "The drama budget is ridiculous, anyway. There are two plays a year, and they both need sets and costumes and lighting people and sound people and musicians. Do you have any idea how much that costs? It's only fair to give some other clubs a turn to work with a big budget."

It's a longer version of what Gianna told me the other day; it's clear now that she was parroting Sydney. And then I remember my first Petition Day, when that girl with the braids came out of the room bubbling over with joy because her request for an expensive telescope was being considered. I think about how petty the Committee is—how petty my sister is—about approving or denying requests that don't require any money at all. And I know this has nothing to do with fairness. This is personal.

My hands clench into fists at my sides. "This doesn't have anything to do with the budget," I say. "Even before Ms. Gutierrez quit, you were trying to sabotage us."

"Was I?" Sydney leans back in her chair and crosses her feet at the ankles, shoving those huge boots in my direction like she's trying to remind me that she could kick my butt. "And what proof do you have of that, exactly?"

"You kept us out of the theater on Monday when we were supposed to have our read-through," I say. "You let Robotics Club have the building, and you put signs and caution tape up everywhere."

"You're the one who petitioned for Robotics Club," Sydney says. "I told you we didn't have the space, but you made such a compelling case, so I gave them the building that made the most sense. They're the ones who put up the signs and the caution tape. I was just doing what *you* asked me to do."

"You could've at least given us a different room," I say.

Sydney shrugs. "I told Maya to contact Grace about it. It's not my fault if she didn't."

I have a feeling that isn't true, but I can't prove it, so I press forward. "You made sure all the pianos in the school would be off-limits that day too. How were we supposed to sing through the score without a piano?"

"We approved a petition for *one* piano to be tuned," Sydney says very slowly and patiently.

"That's the only one that wasn't in use! The band and choir both had rehearsals, and the practice rooms are too small for us to fit in!"

My sister blinks at me slowly. "I don't see how any of that is my fault," she says.

I want very badly to throw something right now. "You made Ms. Gutierrez quit!" I sputter.

Sydney snorts. "She got a part in a Broadway show. How could I possibly have made that happen?"

"I don't know, but I *know* you had something to do with it!"

"I run the Brookside student government," Sydney says deliberately. "I don't control the entire world."

I hate that everything she's saying sounds so reasonable, and I hate that I'm *positive* I'm right but can't prove it, and I hate that the thing I love is being taken away, and I hate that even one single aspect of my life is in my sister's hands. She gets to control literally everyone else at this entire school. Why can't she leave me this one thing?

"You're canceling the play because you don't want me to have it," I say.

The corner of Sydney's mouth quirks up in a humorless smile. "Don't flatter yourself," she says. "The world doesn't revolve around you."

"You've been against me auditioning since the first day of school. That night we went out for pizza with Mom and Dad, you told me there was no way I could *possibly* do it and that I should be in Art Club instead. And then I saw you in the auditorium the day the cast list went up—you looked so irritated when you saw my name up there. You obviously hoped you'd be the only successful one at this school, and you can't *stand* that I've found something I'm good at too and that you're not the only one with a bunch of new friends, so you're trying to take the play away from me—"

"You have no idea what you're talking about," Sydney snaps,

cutting me off. "This argument is pointless. The play is canceled, and there's nothing you can do about it."

"There *is* something I can do about it," I say. "I'll come back on Tuesday with Grace and the other cast members, and we'll petition to have the play reinstated, and—"

"And I'll say no," Sydney says. She picks up her REJECTED stamp and twirls it between her fingers.

"You're not the only one on the Committee. The other girls don't want the play canceled—I talked to them. They'll vote against you, and—"

"They won't vote against me, Abby," my sister says, and when I picture the look on Gianna's face when I asked her why they didn't overrule Sydney, I know it's true. For whatever reason, those girls will rally around my sister regardless of whether it's right.

I stand there silently, cheeks flushed with rage, lava pumping through my veins, and Sydney stares back at me. She looks cool as an ice sculpture. She even looks the tiniest bit bored.

"I think we're done here," she finally says. "There's nothing left for you to do. Go to dinner with all these new friends of yours and leave me alone to do my work."

"We're not done here," I say. "We're not even *close* to done."

I turn on my heel, and I storm out of the Student Government Office.

I blaze across the quad, so angry I'm probably leaving a trail of scorched grass behind me.

I burst into the dining hall, and I spot a table full of my castmates. I march up to them, my eyes and my heart and my blood on fire. This is *not* over. There *is* something left for me to do.

Everyone goes quiet when they see the look on my face.

"Abbi," Grace says. "Are you okay? Did you talk to your sister? What happened?"

I take a deep breath, and then I say, "I'm going to run for the Committee, and then I'm going to save the play. Who wants to help run my campaign?"

Chapter 10

SYDNEY

Just like always, I wake up wishing everyone else would disappear.

Olivia and Hannah are up and dressed, crashing around and giggling like demented hyenas as they gather their stuff for field hockey. They're the ones who get up early for practice, but they also wanted to share the bunks in the inner bedroom, so I'm the one who's stuck sleeping in the bed next to the main door and being disturbed every single morning. I keep asking Vice Principal Rosenberg to put the Committee in charge of rooming decisions, but she keeps saying no, which is extremely annoying. I roll over in a showy way, flapping the blankets around more than necessary so my roommates are sure to notice how irritated I am. Then I pull my pillow over my head, clamp it around my ears, and punctuate the performance with a "hmph."

"Sorry, Sydney," calls one of them, though if they were actually sorry, they'd make at least the tiniest effort not to wake me up. I can't even tell which of them is apologizing. At this point they share pretty much everything, including a voice.

"Bye," the other one says as they head out, or maybe it's the same one. "Have a good day!"

It's weird how people say that so casually, like it's something anyone can do.

I manage to drift back to sleep for almost an hour before my alarm starts blaring. For a few sweet minutes, I allow myself to daydream about staying here all day, alone in my quiet, empty room. But I know I can't. Today is Petition Day, and I am needed.

I tell myself it's as good as being wanted.

I get out of bed and put on my uniform and my lace-up boots, which I always wear on Petition Day. My Dungeons & Dragons character, Capriana the Rogue, wore giant boots, and even though I don't play anymore, dressing like her helps me channel her strength. Capriana started out as chaotic good, always doing what was best for the group, but she never got the respect or the power she deserved until she changed her alignment to evil and learned to rule through fear. She didn't care whether people liked her. She knew you could always cash in on respect.

I created her, so if she can do it, I can do it. I *am* doing it.

I shoulder my backpack and step outside.

Everything is easy while I'm in class. My mind whirs like a well-oiled machine as I sink into the comfortable lull of school-work; I feed my brain information about *Romeo and Juliet* and the Bill of Rights and French vocabulary, and it feeds me correct answers. My hand is at home in the air. When I'm in class, I don't have to think about where to sit. People are eager to be my partner for presentations. Sometimes I can even pretend it's because they want my company, not because they know I'll do more than my share of work.

I don't mind doing extra. I'd rather things be right than fair, and I know they will be if I'm in charge.

And then the end-of-day bell rings, and it's time.

When I arrive at the Student Government Office, there are already ten or twelve petitioners waiting. They shoot me hopeful smiles and flatten themselves against the wall to let me by, and a rush of power sweeps through me from the soles of my boots to the ends of my hair. I think about the time Capriana slaughtered the villagers she was supposed to protect and stole all their money to supply her own group, doling out a little at a time so everyone had what they needed. Was it the *fair* thing to do? Maybe not. But it worked. She made herself indispensable, and nobody could leave her behind unless they wanted to starve. I've worked hard to make myself indispensable here at Brookside, just like Capriana, and nobody can take that away from me. I deserve this.

Lily Zhang, the other eighth-grade representative, is already in her usual seat when I go inside, her long hair brushing the pages of the book she's reading. I predict that it's one of the Chronicles of Wings and Teeth books, and when she flips it shut, I see that I'm right.

"Hey," she says. "Lots of people today, huh?"

"Yeah," I say. I nod at her book. "Any good?"

Her eyes brighten. "So good. This is my fourth time reading it."

"Getting lots of story ideas?" Lily is pretty cool, and she seems to agree with me about Committee stuff most of the time. But just in case she's ever tempted not to vote with me, it's good to give her periodic reminders that I've got copies of her secret fanfic about being in a relationship with Brandozer the dragon.

Lily doesn't respond, but her cheeks flush as she shoves the book into her backpack. I sit down next to her in my special chair and check my phone. I don't have any texts.

The seventh-grade reps, Maya Santos and Gianna Cardelini, show up a few minutes later. It looks like they've been laughing about something, but they put on their serious faces as soon as they join us at the table. This is our fifth Petition Day since school started, but I still haven't gotten used to having only four people on the Committee. It'll feel more balanced once the election happens and we're back up to six.

It'll be exciting to dig up dirt on some new people.

Gianna pulls her usual Ziploc bag of Cinnamon Toast Crunch out of her backpack and starts snacking. She tells everyone she gets it from the dispensers in the dining hall, but I know she steals full industrial-sized boxes from the kitchen and hides them in her closet. I look pointedly at the bag and smile to remind her that her secret is safe with me as long as she votes like I tell her.

"You guys ready to start?" Maya asks. I nod, and she gets up to let the first petitioner in.

Today kicks off with a bunch of easy problems we can solve right away. We grant a maintenance request to fix a broken desk, okay a laptop loan, and give an off-campus pass to a seventh grader I don't know. It's nice when people ask for easy things and I get to feel generous. Two girls present their sides of a dispute involving a group history project, and I tell them we'll talk it over at tomorrow morning's meeting and issue a ruling. Cameron Schwimmer has the stronger case, but I'll make sure we rule in favor of Vivian Hsu. Cameron's one of those totally mediocre girls who gets away with making fun of kids she considers "nerdy" because she's pretty. People like that need to be reminded that they don't have power in any way that matters, and as far as I'm concerned, that's what the Committee is for.

Like I said, I'd rather things be right than fair.

The next petitioner comes in, and I sit up straighter when I see that it's Jenna Aristide. We were partnered up in science class on the first day of seventh grade—my very first day at Brookside—and she treated me like I was any other normal new girl, not one whose parents transferred her to another school because she couldn't manage to keep a single friend at the old one. Of course, I didn't manage to make friends with Jenna either—I acted way too awkward, like always. It didn't take long for her to stop trying, but she still says hi and smiles at me in the halls.

101

I'm pretty satisfied with who I've become at Brookside, but whenever I see her, I wonder if things could've turned out differently.

"Hi, what can we help you with today?" I ask. It's what I say to every petitioner, but with her, I really want to know.

"Hi." Jenna smiles at me as she slides her petition form across the table. It's yellow, which means she wants money for her club. Her long braids are tied back in a ponytail today, and she pulls them over her shoulder and toys with the ends like she's nervous. "I know this is kind of a long shot, especially when you guys just approved our new telescope—thank you so much for that, by the way, it's *awesome*—but I guess you can't win if you don't try, right?"

I take the paper. "Jenna Aristide," I read out loud. "Requesting funds to send Astronomy Club to Cape Canaveral, Florida, to see the launch of the SpaceX Dragon in two months when it departs to deliver a shipment of supplies to the International Space Station. The club has already contacted the Kennedy Space Center, which has agreed to give them a tour and find them a place to watch the launch. Necessary budget for flights, hotels, food, and admission for six students and two chaperones totals seven thousand dollars."

Maya and Gianna exchange a wide-eyed look when I say the number, and Lily almost chokes on her water. People petition for ridiculous things all the time; last week, one girl asked for a flat-screen TV in her dorm room, and another girl asked for a personal shopping budget for the winter dance. But this is probably the most money a six-person club has ever requested.

It's an absurd amount, really, especially after the new telescope.

But I picture how happy Jenna would be, watching that rocket blast off in person.

For one second, I allow myself to imagine standing with her and the rest of Astronomy Club, all of us wearing matching NASA shirts as we follow a bright speck rising into the sky.

I know that's unrealistic. They probably wouldn't want me as part of their group, much less as a friend. And I can't risk asking and being turned down—it might get back to the Committee, and revealing weakness in front of them would destroy everything I've been working toward for a whole year. But Jenna would be so grateful if I could make this trip happen for them. Maybe her gratitude would be enough for me.

"We'll have to talk it over at our meeting tomorrow, but this seems like a great educational opportunity," I say, my face carefully neutral. "Hopefully we can make it work. We'll email you when we decide."

Jenna's eyes light up. "Wow. You'll actually consider it?"

The other three girls stare at me. "We haven't said yes," Lily reminds her.

"But you said maybe, and that's *way* better than no. Thank you so much." Jenna gives me a blinding smile as she turns to go.

We are definitely saying yes.

"We're definitely saying no, right?" says Maya as soon as the door shuts.

"I think we should consider it," I say. I stare her down, giving her plenty of time to remember that I know she once turned in her sister's old English Lit essay instead of writing her own. She knows her perfect GPA can stay intact as long as she cooperates.

She finally looks away and sighs, and I know I've won.

I'm feeling pretty great about myself until Abby walks in.

She looks less like my sister every time I see her. I'm still not used to those squared shoulders, the straight spine, the direct gaze. She walks right up to the table and plunks a pile of papers down in front of me before I can even ask how we can help her today.

"I'm here to submit my paperwork to run for sixth-grade representative," she says, and her voice doesn't shake even a little.

My stomach lurches so hard it's like someone has snagged it with a fishhook and is trying to reel it in. "What?" I say, even though I heard her fine the first time.

"All the signatures are here," she says. She needs fifty to run, and when I flip the pages over, I see that she has collected almost two hundred. That's more than half the school. I have no idea how she managed to get so many signatures in just three days.

I want to tell her she can't run. I'm so used to sitting in this chair and telling people what they're allowed to do. But the Committee can't control who runs for the Committee. All we can do is reject people who don't have their paperwork in order.

"You don't want to do this," I say instead. I force my voice to come out strong, but it takes some serious effort to keep it from trembling.

Abby looks me right in the eyes. "I do, though."

"You know there's a debate, right? You'll have to get up onstage and argue with the other candidates about your platform. The *whole school* will be watching."

Abby grows the tiniest bit paler, but she nods. "I can do it."

There's no way she can do it. She used to cry all through dinner every time she was assigned an oral report, and she'd always back out of giving them at the last minute and accept zeroes. It's obvious she's gotten bolder or she never would've gone through with the play audition, but even that was just for a few people. The debate happens in front of everyone, and if she freaks out, the whole school will laugh at her and remember it forever, like what happened after the third-grade talent show. Abby missed so many class trips and birthday parties and stuff because she wasn't comfortable around the other kids at our old school, but she's been doing so much better here, finally making friends and coming out of her shell. I can't bear to watch her retreat into herself again. I thought I had saved her from that when I canceled the play.

The last time this happened, I stood by and did nothing. Maybe there wasn't much I could have done—it's not like I had any power back then. But this time I definitely do, and I'm not going to stand by and watch her derail her new life.

I pick up the stack of papers and look carefully at the list of signatures. Grace O'Connor, the girl who was supposed to be the assistant director of the play, is listed as Abby's campaign manager, and the first fifteen signatures belong to kids from the cast. "Is this about saving the play?" I ask.

"It's not *just* about that," she says. "But sort of."

"I told you, we don't have the budget this year to—"

"I *know* you have the budget," Abby says. "I tried to reason with you, but you wouldn't listen. This obviously isn't going to get done unless I do it myself."

My sister meets my eyes, a defiant tilt to her chin that I've never seen before, and for a second, all I feel is pride. She's doing exactly what I would do.

And then I'm crushed by the impossibility of the situation. I can't back down and reinstate the play for no apparent reason—if I caved like that, the Committee might get the idea that none of my decisions are truly final. Plus, it wouldn't even guarantee that Abby would withdraw from the race. Even if I could convince her to drop out in exchange for saving the show, the best-case scenario would *still* involve her performing. Nobody can possibly come out ahead here.

Well, except Ms. Gutierrez, I guess. I doubt she would've seen those casting calls for *The Cannibal's Daughter* on Broadway if I hadn't printed them out and put them in her faculty mailbox.

"Sydney?" says Lily, and I realize I've been silent way too long. "Do you want to approve her paperwork, or . . . ?"

I guess I don't have a choice.

I roll the APPROVED stamp across my ink pad and press it

down in the corner of her paperwork, and my stomach twists in protest.

I'm the big sister. It's my responsibility to protect Abby, to make sure she doesn't get hurt, and she's making it absolutely impossible for me to do that.

This is going to end so, so badly.

Chapter 11

Abby's announcement rattles me, and the last thing in the world I want to do is sit in the loud, crowded dining hall. I'd much rather eat in the library with my math homework for company; Ms. Stamos knows I'm careful, so she lets me eat around the books, even sticky stuff like cream cheese and peanut butter. I long for the quiet of my favorite desk by the window, where I can look out over the main quad and keep an eye on what's happening without anyone looking back up at me.

But it's important for me to make an appearance at dinner sometimes. It reminds my classmates that I'm always watching, always listening. So I go.

My first week as president, it was actually exciting to come to the dining hall for every meal. I ate with all the most popular people on a rotating basis, and for a little while, it was exhilarating to know I could plunk my tray down at absolutely any table and no one would turn me away. It's not like the cafeteria at my old school was a minefield or anything, but nobody really talked to me, even if they let me sit where I wanted. But a week ago I spilled a glass of lemonade down my front, and not a single person even laughed. All the girls rushed to hand me napkins, helped wipe off my backpack, and offered me spare shirts as if I didn't have more in my room.

After that I realized I could probably do anything I wanted: eat yogurt with my fingers, wear a giant purple hat, get up on the table and do a tap routine between the plates of half-finished chicken pot pie. It turns out that when you hold everyone's fate in your hands, nobody dares to tease you. I don't know why it took me so long to figure out that I could run my real life like I ran Capriana's pretend one.

Jenna and the Astronomy Club girls are sitting at a table near the windows, and I briefly consider going over and sitting with them. Jenna probably feels pretty friendly toward me now that I've said we'd consider her petition; it seems like she might not mind if I ate some spaghetti next to her for twenty minutes. But I don't want to lead her and the other girls on, and sitting with them might imply that I'm definitely going to send them to Florida when I haven't actually crunched the numbers yet to make sure it's possible. Even if I move all the money from the play over to Astronomy Club, I'll probably still have to siphon some funds away from a few other clubs, and I'm not positive I can make it work.

Plus, even if I were sure about the budget, I don't want

friendliness from Jenna that's purely part of an exchange. I want her to smile at me because she likes me, not just because she thinks I might send her to Cape Canaveral. And since there's no way to tell for sure why someone's being nice to you, it's always better not to get your hopes up. It's impossible to be disappointed that way.

There's an empty spot next to Bree, who runs Environmental Club, so I sit down next to her. She looks startled for a second, but she recovers quickly and scoots over to make room for me. The other girls at the table are deep in conversation, but they break off the moment they see me. At first this kind of thing made me feel powerful; if people weren't legitimately afraid of what I'd do with the facts I gathered, I wouldn't be able to manipulate them. But sometimes it's exhausting to walk through a room and hear girl after girl go quiet like I've muted them with a remote. I'm not *always* looking for information. Sometimes all I want to do is eat my dinner.

All the girls are looking at me nervously, like I'm going to issue some sort of royal proclamation. I wave my hand like I'm trying to swat away a fly, a *Don't pay attention to me* gesture. "Just do what you were doing," I say. "I'm not going to report you."

It's not even remotely funny, but all five of them laugh—since I became president, everyone laughs at my jokes, funny or not. It's like they think I'm keeping a tally of who finds me most amusing. It was nice at first—my actual jokes have always been too weird for most people—but now it just feels kind of sad.

There's a burst of genuine laughter from across the dining hall, and when I turn to look, my eyes land on my sister. She's wearing tight jeans and a bright blue shirt speckled with metallic silver stars—way more eye-catching than anything she ever wore at home—and she's at the very center of a knot of girls, the sun in their solar system. Before we got to Brookside, I don't think I'd ever seen my sister edge past the borders of a group; she didn't even like when we sang to her on her birthday. But now she doesn't look nervous at all.

As I watch, a few people split off from the group, and I see that they're carrying stacks of paper. A tiny girl with white-blond hair stops at the table next to ours and chirps, "Are any of you sixth graders?" When two people say they are, she slides flyers across the table to them. "Hi, my name is Kendall, and I'm campaigning for Abbi Carrington," she says. "I hope you'll consider voting for her for sixth-grade representative. In the few weeks since school started, she's already uncovered all kinds of unfair practices and favoritism inside the Committee that keep students like you from getting the things you want and need. Abbi will do everything she can to restore balance and make sure *your* voices are heard."

The girls pull the flyers toward them. "Cool," says one of them. It's clear none of them has noticed me, but the girls at my own table are exchanging glances and shifting restlessly. They can't believe this is happening right in front of me, and they're half-terrified, half-gleeful, waiting to see what I'll do.

"That's Abbi over there, in the blue shirt," Kendall continues, pointing. "If you have any questions or concerns, she'd be happy to talk to you any time. Or you can just come to next week's debate and listen to her discuss the issues with her opponents."

The reminder makes my stomach ache like there's a tiny monster inside, clawing at the lining, and I suddenly can't sit here silently anymore. I stand, pushing my chair back so hard that it screeches across the wood floor, and stalk over to the next table. I tower over Kendall by a good six inches, and she shrinks down even smaller the moment she registers who I am, her eyes so gigantic they basically take up half her face. I want to snap, *God, I'm not going to hurt you!* but that'll probably scare her more. I smooth over all my frustrations like I'm spreading frosting across the surface of a cake, and when I speak, my voice comes out even. "Can I have one of those?"

Her eyes widen even more. "What?"

I gesture to her chest; she's gripping the flyers close. "One of *those*."

"Oh." Kendall glances over her shoulder at my sister like she's unsure whether she should give me one, but Abby's not looking, so she's forced to make the decision on her own. Finally she peels one off and hands it over, looking at my boots instead of my face.

In bold, black letters, the flyer proclaims, VOTE FOR ABBI CARRINGTON, THE VOICE OF THE PEOPLE! It's still super weird to see my sister's name spelled with an *i*. At the bottom of the page are a few sentences about how much experience she already has petitioning the Committee and how she wants to make sure every student gets the same opportunities. And in the middle is a color photo of her wearing her Brookside uniform and grinning as she leaps into the air, both hands thrown above her head. Her hair is woven into a side-braid, bouncing up from her shoulder. Even though she always wore it down at home, I realize I'm starting to think of this as her signature style.

If I had come across this photo without knowing it was my sister, I'm not totally sure I would've recognized her right away.

I don't know why I'm surprised that a person can reinvent herself at Brookside. It only took me a few weeks here before people realized I paid attention to everything, that I knew secrets they'd been able to hide from everyone else, and started treating me with respect. When one of the girls who'd been elected seventh-grade representative the previous fall moved to Nashville, I beat out Kennedy Howell to replace her with no problem. All I had to do was pay close attention to Kennedy's biggest supporters, learn what they were self-conscious about, and then spread rumors that Kennedy had been making fun of those things behind their backs—nobody trusted her after that. When both seats opened up for eighth-grade representative in the spring, I quietly reported dirt on each of my two opponents to supporters of the other; everyone thought I was on their side, so the other two girls split the vote, but everyone voted for me. It was almost too easy. Nobody even caught on, so I was able to use the exact same trick to secure the presidency at the end of the year. It was almost *too* easy.

So maybe it's not that I'm surprised a person can reinvent herself. Maybe I'm just surprised that Abby could.

Or Abbi, now, I guess.

But no matter how she spells her name, she's still my little sister. When I look at her, a tiny part of me will always see the expression on her face when kids at recess chanted "Crybaby!" at her. I'll always remember the tearful conversation between her and Mom when her grades started dropping because she stopped participating in class, the way she refused to try out for choir even though she has a really good voice.

I have to step up and do something before she hurtles straight into disaster again.

❌ ✖ ✖

Chapter 12

When Abby gets out of social studies at the end of the next day, I'm standing outside the classroom waiting for her. (I told my math teacher I needed to leave early to do something for the Committee, and he let me go with no questions asked.) My sister is chatting animatedly with another girl, but when she sees me, her smile flattens. "You go ahead," I hear her say, and then she takes a deep breath before marching up to me. Normally I'm happy that people need to steel themselves before confronting me, but this time it hurts a little.

"What are you doing here?" she asks.

"Hello to you too," I say. "We need to talk."

She sticks her chin out. "I'm not dropping out of the race, if that's what you—"

"That's not what I'm going to say," I interrupt. "Come on. Follow me."

And to my surprise, she does.

We don't talk as I lead her to the Student Center. There are a few girls hanging out on the couches, but the Student Government Office is pretty soundproof, and their voices go quiet when I shut the door. I'm drawn to my normal seat, where I feel powerful and safe, but I don't want to scare Abby off, so I perch on the edge of the table instead.

"The debate with all the sixth-grade candidates is next Wednesday—" I start.

Abby rolls her eyes. "Yeah, I *know*."

"—and I want to make sure you're prepared."

My sister opens her mouth, but the argument dies in her throat when she registers what I've said. "Why do *you* care? I know you don't want me to win."

It's true, but I just say, "I want you to have a fair chance."

Abby snorts. "Since when do *you* care about fairness?"

Why is she making it so difficult to help her? "You don't want people to think you're getting special privileges because you're related to me, do you?" I say—riling her up will make her want to prove herself. "Don't you want to show everyone you can hold your own?"

As I hoped, her cheeks get pinker. "I can hold my own just fine. I don't need your help. I know you're trying to—"

I cut her off. "Show me that you're ready, and I'll back off and leave you alone."

She side-eyes me. "How?"

"Easy. I'll sit over there, and you'll stand here, and I'll give you a question, and you'll answer it." She still has that suspicious look on her face, so I say, "God, Abby, I'm not trying to trick you. Just do it, okay? If you really are prepared, it won't be a big deal, and you can go tell everyone how annoying I am."

"*Fine,*" she says.

I sit down behind the table in Lily's usual chair, and Abby plants herself on the spot I indicated. Once she's there, she looks a little less sure of herself. I sit quietly and watch her for a minute, and after a few seconds, her hand flies up to her hair, and she starts twisting it around her fingers like she always used to do at home when she was nervous. She notices herself doing it, forces her hand down, and glowers at me.

"So are you going to ask me a question or what?" she asks.

"Abby," I say, "why are you more qualified to be the sixth-grade representative than Samantha, Kylee, or Angelina?" It's a no-brainer question, one she must've been thinking about a lot.

"Um. I. Um." Abby starts to curl into herself and tuck her hands into her pockets, but she immediately realizes what she's doing and pulls them out. One hand flies up to her braid again, then drops, and I can see how hard she's working to keep it at her side. She arranges her shoulders into this stiff, tilted position and sticks her chin out in a way she probably thinks looks cool and confident. Mostly she looks like a nutcracker someone has dropped on the floor one too many times.

"Well," she starts again, and then she does this extremely weird laugh, high and manic. "Well. I've, um, I've been up

117

against . . . I've been *in front of* the Committee lots of times already, asking for stuff, for petitions, for me and for other people, like a proxy? So I . . . I think . . . Other people don't have the experience with the Committee that I have, unless they've petitioned for stuff every week, which I don't think they have." She laughs again and tosses her braid over her shoulder in this bizarre, affected way, like she's trying to copy a dance move from a music video. Since the braid is meant to be on the side of her head, it bounces right back.

It would be so easy to just let her fail—then all of this would go away. The play would stay canceled, and Abby wouldn't get in the way of how I run my Committee. But the whole point was to save her from humiliation, to make sure she continues to have lots of opportunities here, and letting her get up onstage at the debate and do *this* would mean humiliation of the highest degree.

"Stop," I say, and she deflates. "What are you *doing*?"

"I'm answering the question," Abby says, but her voice is small.

"Okay, first of all, why are you standing like that?"

"This is how she stands," my sister says, and then her eyes widen like she wishes she could cram the words back into her mouth. "I. This is how *I*—"

"Who's *she*?" I say. "Who stands like that?"

"Abbi does," she mumbles.

"Who? Are you talking about yourself in the third person?"

"No, it's . . . *Abbi*, with an *i*," she says a little louder. "That's

118

who I am now. Here. At Brookside." Mottled red creeps up from under the collar of her shirt and pools in her cheeks.

And suddenly I understand. My sister didn't just change the spelling of her name. She's playing a character. That's why everything is different: her voice, her stance, her clothes, the way she laughs, the activities she's joining. She's not trying to be a reinvented version of herself, like I am—she's trying to be someone else entirely. And whoever that person is, she can't handle this debate any better than my regular sister can.

"So you're her all the time now?" I ask. "Even when you're in class? Or with your friends?" She nods. "Doesn't that get exhausting?"

Her shoulders droop. "Honestly? Yeah. I've been so tired lately."

"Then why are you doing it? Why bother?"

She stares at me like it's obvious. "You know why."

"Tell me anyway."

She squirms. "Because . . . it's just . . . it's easier. I mean, Abbi has friends. Like, lots of them. People really like her. And she's brave. There are a lot of things I can't do, but she can do all of them. Or almost all of them."

"Yeah, no," I say. "It's not 'Abbi' who can do those things. It's you."

"It's *not*," she says. "People don't even know me. And if they did, they wouldn't . . ." She starts winding her braid around her finger again. "It's just that she can't do this *one thing*, making stuff up on the spot. She couldn't do it during Freeze at rehearsal, and she can't do it now, and—"

"Okay, seriously you've got to stop with this 'she' thing," I say.

"But—"

"No. You own your failures, you own your successes. There isn't anyone else."

"Fine." Abby drops her gaze to her shoes. "*I* can't do this one thing, then. Are you happy now?"

"I think you probably can do it, though," I say. "You just don't know how yet. Fortunately you've got a sister who does, because she's done this before, twice."

She crosses her arms over her chest. "You can't magically give me the ability to improvise."

"This isn't about improvising. It's about preparation and practice."

Abby looks up, and a tiny spark of hope ignites in her eyes. If she managed to get a part in the play, preparation and practice are things she knows all about. "But how am I supposed to prepare answers when I don't know what the questions are going to be?"

"I can tell you what they were last year and the year before. And even if there's a new question you don't expect, there are always ways to steer the conversation back to something you want to talk about."

"Huh," she says. It looks like she honestly hasn't thought of this before.

I pull a notebook out of my backpack. "Come here. We're going to make you some talking points."

My sister slinks over and slides into the chair next to mine, feet tucked around the legs the way she used to sit at the dinner table. "I *really* don't get why you're doing this."

"Everyone knows we're related," I say. "It reflects badly on me if you're unprepared. And people probably assume I'm helping you anyway. Might as well actually do it, right?"

She nods like she accepts that, and we get to work.

For the next half hour, Abby and I talk through the questions Vice Principal Rosenberg has asked in the past. *What makes you most qualified to be the sixth-grade representative? Why is it important for students to govern themselves? How do you think the Committee can serve students most effectively? What's one thing you'd like to accomplish if you were elected?* My sister has good ideas, but she's hesitant to speak up at first, since a lot of her answers have to do with saving the play and making sure I run the Committee more fairly. She seems afraid that I might use the information she's giving me against her, but when I remind her that I don't have control over how the sixth graders vote, she seems to relax.

To be honest, I probably *could* control how the sixth graders vote. But as fun as it would be, I don't have time to gently steer one hundred and twenty girls toward the outcome I want by next week.

When the talking points are done, I tear out the page and hand it to her. "Memorize these," I say. "Practice saying them over and over until you can do it in your sleep. You can bring pretty much any question Vice Principal Rosenberg asks you back around to these points. If you don't think you can remember them, you can write them on notecards and—"

"Of course I can remember them," Abby says, scowling at me. "I memorized every song in *Cinderella* in like two days."

Being angry is good for her confidence, so I don't argue. "Okay. Now get up, and we'll work on your delivery."

Abby returns to her spot on the floor, shoulders back in that weird tilt and nutcracker chin on full display. "No," I say, frustrated. "Just stand like yourself."

"This *is* like myself," Abby insists. After weeks of playing this character every waking minute, it seems like she's literally forgotten how to be regular Abby.

I stalk over to her, take her by the upper arms, and shake her gently until her spine and neck and shoulders relax and her arms flop by her sides. I push her shoulders back, tilt her chin up a normal amount, and survey my work. She looks supported but not wooden, confident but not bizarre. "Perfect," I say. "Can you remember how this feels?"

"It feels . . . weird." She wiggles her shoulders. "I really look normal right now? I feel like I have crazy monkey arms."

"You don't have crazy monkey arms, whatever that means." I snap a photo of her with my phone and hold it up. "See? Totally normal."

She peers at it. "Oh," she says. "Huh."

"Okay, let's try again." I sit back down. "Abby, why are you uniquely qualified to represent the sixth grade on the Committee?"

My sister holds her posture, but her hand flies up to flip her braid, and that same manic laugh tumbles out of her mouth. *"No,"* I say before she can even get a word out.

She rolls her eyes. "What *now*? I'm standing like you told me to."

"Stop with the Abbi affectations. All of them. No laughing, no playing with your hair. It looks ridiculous, and you don't need to fill the silence while you think about what you're going to say. If you need to get your thoughts together, just *be quiet* and take a deep breath. It'll probably feel like it takes forever, but it'll only be a few seconds. It'll also give you more time to think if you repeat the question back to the moderator. Like, if she were to ask you, 'Why are you wearing a blue sweater?' you'd say, 'I'm wearing a blue sweater because blue is my favorite color.' Got it?"

"Yeah, okay." Abby sighs. "I don't know if I can do this without being her."

And I sympathize. I really do. I remember all too well how pretending to be someone else can help you deal with problems in your life without having to confront them head-on. When I used to go to Josh's house to play D&D and got to be Capriana the Rogue, it was the only time I actually felt strong and brave. The whole week of awkward interactions at school would fall away, and for a few glorious hours, everything felt possible. But now I don't need to be Capriana. I'm just a stronger version of myself, and I still hold everyone at this school in the palm of my hand.

"You're a good actress," I tell my sister. "You've been playing this Abbi-with-an-*i* character since you got here, and I guess that's worked out pretty well so far. But Abbi's not right for this debate, so you need to play a different character. Try

123

pretending to be a version of yourself who's really good at debating, okay? Play Abby-with-a-y, but in an alternate universe where you're not afraid."

My sister closes her eyes and stands very still; she seems to be searching for something deep inside herself. Finally she opens her eyes and nods. "Okay," she says. "Ask me again."

"Abby, what makes you uniquely qualified to represent the sixth grade?"

I can see an Abbi laugh bubbling up in her throat, but my sister takes control and swallows it down. She breathes deeply in and out, like I said. She glances at the paper in her hand. And when she speaks, she sounds like herself in the best possible way.

"I'm uniquely qualified to represent the sixth grade because I've already had a lot of experience interacting with the Committee," she says. "I went to my first Petition Day on the second day of school, and because it went so well, a lot of people have asked me to present petitions for them as a proxy. I've been to every Petition Day since, and I've never had a petition rejected, and I've learned a lot about how the Committee works. Now I'm ready to take the next step and become a voting member. I want to help my fellow students get the things they need from the other side." When she's done, she breaks into a genuine smile of delighted surprise.

"*Good,*" I say. "That was perfect. Practice doing all your answers exactly like that, and you won't have any trouble."

"Okay. Yeah. I will." Abby looks down at the paper in her hands, then back up at me, a little shyer now. "Thank you. You didn't have to help me."

And suddenly I feel shy and awkward too. It's not something I've felt in a long time, and it catches me off guard. I lean down and fiddle with the laces of my boot so I don't have to meet her eyes.

"Don't get used to it," I say. "This was a one-time thing. If you win and you keep trying to take me down, it's going to be war between us."

When I look up again, she's smiling. "That's more like it," she says. "I was wondering what you'd done with my sister."

Chapter 13

SYDNEY

For the next week, nobody talks about anything but the debate. The other Committee girls are totally obsessed; they spend every moment trying to guess who the sixth graders will choose. I guess it makes sense—we're going to be spending a ton of time with whoever wins—but I'm so anxious that their chatter grates on my nerves. Nobody dares to say anything bad about Abby in front of me, but it seems like Angelina is everyone's favorite because her posters are so funny. I drop hints in meetings and at dinner that I think Samantha seems like a strong candidate too, and everyone around me nods, obviously taking note. With any luck, that unofficial endorsement will get around to the sixth graders and Sam and Angelina will knock my sister out of the race.

Every time I walk into a classroom building or the Student

Center or the gym or the dining hall, my eyeballs are assaulted by brightly colored, glitter-splashed posters screaming, VOTE FOR KYLEE and SAM IS YOUR FAM and ANGELINA HAS SUPERPOWERS (NOT REALLY BUT VOTE FOR HER ANYWAY). My sister's grinning face stares back at me from wall after wall: VOTE FOR ABBI, THE VOICE OF THE PEOPLE.

I can only hope the people won't listen.

I spend practically every lunch period in the library. It's mostly because Ms. Stamos has declared it a "campaign-free zone," but if I'm honest with myself, it's also because I know Jenna has study hall right before lunch. On the day after I email her to say we've found the money to send her club to Cape Canaveral—at the expense of the play, the dance team, and the soccer team, but she doesn't have to know that—I manage to time things exactly right and run into her. She beams at me and says, "Sydney, thank you so, so much for approving our petition. We can't wait to go. You've totally made our year."

I tell her I'm glad I could help and that I hope it's fun, and she says, "You're seriously the best." Her shoulder bumps mine as she turns to go, and she laughs and puts her hand on my arm and says, "Oh, sorry," like I'm just another regular girl, maybe even the kind of person she could be friends with.

For the rest of that day, nothing can touch me.

But even that can't stop time from moving forward. Way before I'm ready, it's debate day, and I'm sitting in the front row of the auditorium flanked by Maya, Lily, and Gianna. They're all wriggling with excitement, and my stomach wriggles right along with them. I can't stop picturing Abby backstage, winding her braid around her finger and taking quick, shallow breaths. Has she been practicing enough? Has she changed her mind about wanting to go through with this? Is the next hour going to be a horrifying, drawn-out repeat of the third-grade talent show?

I so clearly remember sitting in the auditorium of King Elementary, frozen with horror as I watched Abby miss her cue to start singing "Castle on a Cloud." A look of pure terror swept over her face, and then her chin started trembling the way it always did when she was little and Mom told her it was time to turn off the TV and take a bath. I focused on her as hard as I could, trying to send her a telepathic message that she should just pick up at the start of the next verse. *You can still save yourself!* I screamed at her inside my head. But she didn't, or maybe she couldn't. Instead she started to sob. It was probably only twenty seconds before a teacher escorted her offstage, but it felt like a thousand years.

Tabitha Anderson, who was sitting next to me, turned and said, "Isn't that your sister? What's *wrong* with her?"

"Who knows?" I said. "She's kind of a freak."

Now I pull out my phone and text Abby. *Are you ready?*

She writes back immediately. *I think so.*

Good luck, I write. *Do it like we practiced, and it's going to go great.*

Thanks, she answers, and that's it. That's all I can do.

It's not nearly enough.

The lights in the auditorium go down, and Vice Principal

Rosenberg comes out of the wings with a microphone. Seeing her sends a ping of nervous energy through me, just like always. She's technically the Committee's faculty advisor, and I've already had to dodge her a bunch of times when she wanted to be more involved in our business than was comfortable for me—that is to say, involved at all. I've managed to fend off her requests to come to our meetings, giving her the bare minimum of information and stressing how important it is for the Committee to be a safe, adult-free space for students. She's so into the idea of us governing ourselves that she has bought into it so far; I've even been able to smooth things over when a few girls had the guts to complain to the administration that their petitions had been "unfairly" rejected. But it makes me jumpy every time I remember that there's someone who wants to supervise us.

"Good afternoon, young women of Brookside," she says now, her super-enthusiastic voice booming to the back of the auditorium. She's so hyped up that she's practically bouncing out of her pumps. "We're about to take part in the most sacred of democratic traditions: electing our new representatives. Here's how today will work. First each of our candidates will introduce herself to you, and then I'll ask them a series of questions, some of which come from me and some of which I've collected from the sixth graders. Each candidate will have ninety seconds to answer. When the debate is over, our sixth graders will move down to the polling station in the dance studio in an orderly fashion. Seventh and eighth graders will not be voting today, as they elected their representatives last spring, but I so appreciate those of you who have come out to support your fellow students."

"Go Angelina!" someone shouts from the back row, and a wave of giggles sweeps through the auditorium.

"That brings me to my final point," Vice Principal Rosenberg says. "I'm delighted by how invested you are in your candidates' success. But after our initial round of applause, it's important that you remain quiet until the end of the debate. The best way to help these four young women right now is to let them focus, and then you can show them some love at the polls. The administration will count the votes during dinner, and we'll announce the winners by email at eight o'clock.

"Is everyone ready?"

A wave of cheering rises up around me. My hands feel heavy and tingly with nerves at the same time, but I know people are looking at me, so I force myself to clap.

"Then here we go," says Vice Principal Rosenberg. "It's my pleasure to introduce your candidates for sixth-grade representative: Samantha Bannockburn, Abbi Carrington, Kylee Cho, and Angelina Walker!"

Everyone screams again as the four girls walk out onstage, smiling and waving as they head toward the semicircle of chairs arranged around a microphone. All of them are wearing their uniforms, but they each have an accessory that makes them look unique. My sister has on a pair of bright pink knee socks covered in stars that I've never seen before. She sits in the second chair from the left and crosses her legs. I'm sure she must be incredibly nervous, but she's hiding it well. All the other girls are fidgeting, jiggling a foot or twisting a bracelet around and around, but Abby is completely still. I cross my fingers and hope it means she's calm, not paralyzed with fear.

"Hi there, candidates," Vice Principal Rosenberg says. "To start us off, I'd like each of you to come up to the mic and introduce yourselves. This isn't about telling us your ideas for the Committee—just let us know who you are, where you're from, what your hobbies are, and anything else you'd like to say. Samantha, why don't you start, and we'll proceed in alphabetical order."

Samantha stands up. She's wearing Converse sneakers covered in purple sequins, and they glitter in the light as she approaches the mic. She starts talking, but it's impossible to pay attention to anything she's saying, knowing that Abby's up next. In thirty seconds, my sister will be standing at that mic, facing the whole student body. What if she tries to talk and no sound comes out? What if she cries?

She has so much time left at Brookside. So much time to be teased.

"Thanks, Samantha," says Vice Principal Rosenberg. "Abbi?"

For a minute, my sister doesn't stand up. Her face doesn't even change, like she hasn't noticed someone is speaking to her, and I think, *Oh god, she really is frozen*. I slide to the edge of my seat, ready to leap up, though I know there's nothing I can do to save her. But then I see her chest move slowly up and down, and I realize she's just following my instructions.

She's preparing. And then she stands up, smooths her skirt, and walks to the mic. Her head is up, her shoulders are back, and her arms are relaxed. She looks like Abby, not Abbi.

"Hi, everyone," she says in her normal voice. "My name is Abby Carrington, and I'm from Somerville, Massachusetts, and I'm so excited to be running for sixth-grade representative. I love singing and acting. At my old school, I was in Art Club, and I especially like painting with acrylics. I love graphic novels and *Moana* and cats and going to the beach in Maine with my family, and I hope you'll let me represent you on the Committee this year!"

She turns around and walks back to her seat, totally confident, and I let out a sigh of relief so loud that Lily glances over at me. But I can't help it. My sister is *doing* it. She practiced giving her answers like I showed her, and this isn't going to be a disaster of epic proportions.

Of course, it will be if she wins. But I'll deal with that later. For now I can breathe.

When everyone is done with their introductions, Vice Principal Rosenberg asks the obvious first question: Why are you uniquely qualified to represent the sixth grade? She asks Abby to go first, and this time my sister doesn't even pause. She's on her feet in a second and bounds up to the mic like she's eager to give her answer. "Angelina says on her posters that she has superpowers," she begins. "But I have a superpower none of my fellow candidates have: experience dealing with the Committee." She goes on to give the answer we practiced last week, embellished with accounts of how she has already helped fight for things that will affect the whole school, like more vegetarian options in the cafeteria. Her delivery seems so natural that I can tell she's been practicing a lot.

"And I'm unique in my passion too," she continues. "A few weeks ago, I auditioned for the fall play, and I landed a part. I've never been in a play before, and I was super excited to try it. But then the Committee canceled it, which I believe is completely unjust."

A group of theater girls is sitting near me, and one of them shouts, "Yeah!" then claps her hand over her mouth. "Sorry," she stage-whispers, and everyone laughs, including Abby. It's her normal laugh, not her high, manic Abbi laugh.

"Thanks, Lydia," she says into the mic, totally casual, like she's used to having friends cheer for her. "Anyway, if you elect me as your representative, I will do absolutely everything I can to have the play restored, and I will fight just as hard for every other student who has something unfairly snatched away from her."

I'm actually surprised by how diplomatic she's being. I expected her to get up onstage and call me out personally. Against all odds, my sister is a great politician.

Vice Principal Rosenberg asks a lot of the questions I thought she'd ask, and Abby fields them all really well. She fumbles a bit more on the ones we didn't practice—once she even pulls her braid over her shoulder and twists it as she thinks—but she muddles through. Angelina is super prepared too; she seems a little less friendly than Abby, a bit more ruthless. I don't feel like I have a good enough handle on her to control her, and that scares me. But if she gets elected, I'll consider it a challenge. If you dig deep enough into anything, you're sure to hit dirt eventually.

Samantha is charismatic and funny, but her answers meander so much that she passes the ninety-second mark every single time, and when Vice Principal Rosenberg stops her, she goes, "But wait, I just want to say one more thing . . ." Kylee is a total mess—all her answers basically boil down to "I want to be on student government because . . . I want to." I hope everyone votes for her. I bet I could get her to do what I want even without digging up dirt on her.

Vice Principal Rosenberg moves on to questions the other sixth graders have submitted. Most of them are super specific, like, "If I petitioned for two hundred dollars for my club, would you approve it?" It gets boring after a while, but Vice Principal Rosenberg patiently works her way through a bunch of them, including the one that says, "What's your favorite kind of cheese?" When Abby gets to the mic, she says, "Does the cheese powder on Doritos count?" and everyone laughs.

I'm surprised to find that I'm not sitting on the edge of my seat anymore.

And then the whole thing is abruptly over. "Please give our candidates a huge round of applause," our vice principal says, and everyone lets out all the enthusiasm they've been bottling up. I watched a bunch of political debates to prepare before I ran for the Committee last year, and I know that the candidates should all shake hands now. But these girls awkwardly stand up and look around, then grab one another's hands and take a bow. Abby stands toward the middle, beaming as everyone claps.

I guess it's only fair that she should get a chance to bow in front of a cheering crowd, since I took the play away from her.

The candidates head offstage, and the noise level sky-rockets as the seventh and eighth graders make their way out of the auditorium and the sixth graders line up to head down-stairs. Since the Committee is in the front row, we'll be the last ones out.

Gianna nudges me as we wait to exit our row. "Your sister did awesome," she says.

"She really did," says Lily, and Maya nods in agreement.

I know they would tell me Abby was great regardless of what happened up on that stage, but the thing is, she really was. There wasn't even one moment when she verged on making a fool of herself, and part of me is dizzy with relief.

But by proving that she can handle herself in front of a crowd, my sister has also proven that I canceled the play for absolutely no reason. I didn't need to protect her; all I've done is take away something she loves. And now, no matter what happens, I can't give it back without making myself look weak.

Before, fighting my sister was about doing what was best for her. But now it's about upholding my reputation as a strong president.

If one of us falls, it has to be her.

Chapter 14

SYDNEY

The email goes out at exactly eight o'clock, like Vice Principal Rosenberg promised.

It is my pleasure to announce that the two sixth graders who will serve on the Brookside Academy Student Representative Officers Committee are Angelina Walker and Abbi Carrington. Congratulations to all our candidates on a wonderful campaign and debate. As always, I'm so inspired by the intelligence, persistence, and bravery shown by the young women of Brookside. Thanks are also due to the rest of the sixth-grade class, who took part in the sacred American tradition of electing our leaders democratically. It is so important to vote and make your voices heard, and I hope you do so with pride at every opportunity for the rest of your lives!

It's not like I'm surprised—Angelina and Abby were clearly the best candidates. But I still feel like I have a rock in the pit of my stomach, and I know it'll be there a good long while.

Loud music starts blasting from the quad—it's that cheesy "Celebrate good times, come on!" song that my dad likes—followed by peals of laughter. When I peer out the window, I spot Grace O'Connor parading across the lawn, holding a wireless speaker aloft with one hand and leading my sister by the other. A whole bunch of girls follow them, cheering and waving their hands in the air. When they reach the middle of the quad, Grace sets down the speaker, and the girls form a dancing, whooping circle around her and Abby.

Old Abby would've been traumatized into silence for the next week by this kind of display. But as I watch, my sister takes Grace's hand and lets her friend spin her around. I catch a glimpse of her upturned face for a moment as she whirls, and I see that she's laughing.

A tiny part of me wonders what it would be like to have a friend spin me around.

I close the blinds, crack my knuckles, and get to work. I have more important things to do.

I open all my social media accounts and search for Angelina Walker. She doesn't seem to have Facebook, but I find her Instagram account after a few tries. However, she only has seven pictures posted: five of her cat, one of a doughnut, and one selfie in a pair of giant sunglasses. There's nothing here I can use.

Instead I log into the Brookside website and pull up the student directory. Angelina's picture is third from the bottom of the sixth-grade class. The generic blue background makes me think it's her school picture from last year, and her hair is in cornrows with beads on the ends instead of the twists she has now. I find her hometown, then search the whole directory for Kingston, Rhode Island.

My heart does a little twirl when I get a second match. There's another sixth grader from Kingston named Katie Radner. Jackpot.

I send Katie an email. *Hi. My name is Sydney, and I'm the president of the Committee. Quick question for you: Did you know Angelina Walker before you came to Brookside?*

A reply comes almost immediately. *Yeah, we went to the same church. We're not really friends though. Why?*

A tiny part of me is actually disappointed—it's almost not fun when a source falls right into your lap with no effort at all. But it's not like I'm going to turn it down, so I write back, *Can you meet me in the Student Center in fifteen minutes?*

She replies, *Am I in trouble or something?*

I send back one final message: *No, of course not. I just want to talk to you.* And then I grab my bag and head across the quad. I make sure to go out the back door of my dorm, the one that doesn't face Abby's celebratory dance party.

The Student Center is completely empty, so I sit down on one of the couches instead of waiting in the Student Government Office. All the furniture in here is pretty disgusting—we should allocate some money toward getting new couches. Then again, we can barely afford to send Astronomy Club to Cape Canaveral, and that's obviously more important.

Katie arrives right on time, shifty-eyed behind her bright pink glasses. She's got her hoodie sleeves pulled all the way over her hands like she's trying to protect them, and I feel kind of bad that I've made her so nervous. But there's no reason to be sorry, really. If everything goes like I think it will, she and I will both have something we want by the end of this conversation.

My instinct is to stand up to greet her, but I force myself to stay seated so I look less intimidating. I probably should've changed out of my Capriana boots. "Hi," I say in my gentlest voice. "I'm Sydney. Want to come sit down?"

"Okay," Katie says. She crams herself into the opposite corner of the sofa, knees pulled up in front of her. She's small for her age, and she's wearing tiny pink Keds that match her glasses. "Did something, like, happen to Angelina? Because I don't know anything about that."

"No, nothing like that," I say. "I was hoping you and I could make a deal. I think you might have something I want, and I'm pretty sure I can offer you something you want in return."

Now she looks completely bewildered. "What things?"

"Do you know how Petition Day works, Katie?"

She nods, obviously relieved to be back on a subject she understands. "If we want something, we fill out a form, and then we come and ask you guys to approve it? And then you vote on whether we can have it? My RA told us."

"That's exactly right," I say. "So, this is what I'm thinking. If you can tell me something embarrassing about Angelina that happened back in Kingston, something she wouldn't want anyone at Brookside to know, I promise to get three petitions approved for you this year. They can be anything you want, within reason—I can't get you a thousand dollars of personal spending money or anything, but off-campus passes, budget approvals for clubs, a pizza party for you and your friends . . . Whatever you want, I'll make it happen."

Katie's eyes widen. "Really?"

"If you can give me the information I need, yes. Really."

"But if something embarrassing about Angelina gets out and then I show up at Petition Day and get whatever I want, won't she know it was me? She's on the Committee now."

Huh. Katie's smarter than I thought. "How about this," I say. "When you want something, fill out a form and slip it under my door. I'm in Bryant, room 309. I'll authorize it myself. Nobody else has to know."

"Yeah, all right." Katie bites her thumbnail, considering. "Can you get me a mini fridge in my dorm room?"

"Absolutely."

A smile creeps over her face, and she leans forward. "I'm not allowed to have soda at home, but my big sister said she'd order some cases of Cherry Coke for me online. She's in college."

"I can definitely make sure your Cherry Coke is cold," I say, though I can't imagine why anyone would want to drink *that* of all things. "Now, I want you to think very carefully about

140

Angelina. Tell me anything at all that you think might be embarrassing—there's no wrong answer here. You can take as much time as you need."

"I don't need time," Katie says, eager now. "So, okay. Angelina and I were in the same youth group last year, and there was this boy, Brad? He was in seventh grade, and Angelina was totally in love with him. She wrote him this suuuuuper, long letter, like *six pages* of gushing about his favorite TV show and his favorite sports teams and how cute his dog was and how much she liked his shoes. And this girl Gabby was going through Angelina's bag looking for lip gloss or something, and she found the letter and took photos of it, and by the next day everyone in the entire youth group had seen it. Angelina was so embarrassed that she stopped coming to youth group for a month. She tried to pretend she had the stomach flu, but some of the other girls said she was still going to school, and nobody gets the stomach flu for a *month*."

Wow—I didn't expect anything this good. "Gabby sent it to *everyone*?" I ask, trying not to betray my excitement.

Katie nods. "She loved drama. She was always telling people stuff other people had said about them and trying to get them to fight."

"Do you still have the photos?"

"Maybe." Katie pulls out her phone—the case has an anime character on the back—and spends a while tapping and scrolling. Finally she says, "Oh, here," and my heart leaps. I reach for the phone, but she doesn't hand it over. "You *promise* I'm not going to get in trouble? Nobody will know I gave this to you?"

"I promise," I say. "It'll never come back to you. Just think of all those cold Cherry Cokes."

She lets go.

I skim the letter, which is exactly as Katie described, then send it to myself and delete the message from Katie's phone. I'll print a few hard copies when I get to my room and hide them in the air vent so there won't be any evidence in my email. "Thank you," I say as I hand back her phone. "You've been a really huge help. I'll expect to see that fridge request form under my door soon, okay?"

Katie tucks her phone into the pocket of her oversized hoodie—it's a lot like the ones Abby used to wear. "So . . . that's it?" she asks.

"That's it. You're free to go."

"I . . . Great, um, okay." Katie stands uncertainly. "Bye, I guess?"

"Have a great night." She turns to go, and I say, "Oh, and Katie? Obviously our deal is off if you tell anyone about this conversation. And I will know if you do."

"Right, yeah," she says, and then she's gone. The way she skitters out of the Student Center reminds me of a frightened squirrel darting up a tree.

I take my phone into the Student Government Office, the place I feel safest, and lock the door behind me. I take my place in my special chair, and I read the letter twice. Angelina spends an entire paragraph on how "adorable" it is that Brad's hair and his dog are the same color, and she says that her heart "glows like a star" when she knows she and Brad are home watching *Hungry for Brains* at the same time. Katie was right about how much Angelina mentions Brad's shoes; those must've been some seriously amazing sneakers.

The whole thing is a total train wreck, which means it's a gold mine for me.

• • •

The next morning, I get to breakfast super early and wait in an inconspicuous corner by the entrance until Angelina arrives with three friends. I silently follow them across the dining hall and into the serving area, knowing it won't be long before she's alone. Most girls go for the eggs and bacon and French toast, which are in chafing dishes along the left wall, but I've noticed that Angelina is one of the few people who actually likes eating oatmeal for breakfast. As soon as she approaches the vat near the salad bar, I sidle up next to her. "Hi, Angelina," I say.

My new Committee member jumps—she clearly didn't hear me approach—and oatmeal sloshes over the rim of the ladle and splats against the floor. "You scared me," she says.

"I didn't mean to startle you," I say, even though I did. "I just wanted to congratulate you on the election. Oh, and to give you this."

I carefully angle my body so nobody else can see what I'm doing, then remove a piece of paper from the inside pocket of my blazer and slide it onto her tray. Angelina unfolds it, and I watch her eyes widen as she registers her fifth-grade self's handwriting. "What . . ." she sputters. "Where did this . . . How—"

"You don't have to be scared," I say in a low, soothing tone that won't be heard over the noise of rattling dishes and laughing girls. "Nobody else has to know about this. Trust me, I'm *great* at keeping secrets. All I need in return is to know you'll back me up when the Committee votes."

"Votes on what?"

I shrug. "On everything."

"But . . ." Angelina looks around wildly like someone might be able to save her, but her friends are still serving themselves, and nobody's paying any attention to us. When she speaks again, her voice is even lower. "How did you even get this?"

I shrug. "It's amazing what you can find on the internet, isn't it?"

"It's on the *internet*? But—"

"Don't worry, it's not easy to find. And nobody at Brookside would even know to search for it, right?" I toy innocently with my backpack strap. "Unless someone told them, that is."

Angelina's starting to look a little green. "Are you saying—"

"I'm saying I have a feeling you and I are going to work really well together." I squeeze her shoulder, and she flinches. "Have a good breakfast, and I'll see you at your first Committee meeting."

I walk away, and I feel Angelina's eyes on my back all the way across the serving area as I stick two pieces of bread into the toaster. When I check over my shoulder a minute later, she's ripping the paper I handed her into tiny pieces, which she stuffs into her oatmeal and dumps into the trash. One of her friends approaches her and asks a question, and I hear her mutter that she's not hungry anymore.

I take my tray into the dining hall and sit down to eat my breakfast, my heart glowing like a star.

✗ ✗ ✗

Chapter 15

It takes a few days for the administration to rearrange Angelina's and Abby's schedules, so their first meeting with us is the following Tuesday's Petition Day. Vice Principal Rosenberg tells us that the sixth graders should spend their first day watching us debate and vote, and on Wednesday morning, once they have a sense of how the Committee works, they should be allowed to dive in as full voting members. She offers to sit in on our new members' first meeting so she can welcome them herself, but I manage to fend her off by telling her we have a lot of work to get through.

Lily, Maya, and Gianna seem super excited when the new girls arrive—they pull out chairs for them and fall all over themselves to be welcoming. Gianna has even brought chocolate chip muffins, which I'll admit is a nice touch, even though they're just the normal ones from the dining hall that she's saved from breakfast. It's almost like the other girls think having new blood in the room is going to make things different.

"Wow, Gianna, you're seriously an expert at getting food out of the dining hall without anyone noticing," I say. I feel the tiniest bit bad about it, since I plan to have a muffin myself, but it's important to remind the rest of them that I haven't forgotten their secrets.

Gianna's face goes red. "I *asked* if I could take these," she grumbles, and I know she's gotten the message.

Angelina meets my eyes for a moment as she settles into her seat, just long enough for me to see the fear there, then drops her gaze submissively to the floor. Abby, on the other hand, looks straight at me and smiles. It's definitely not the kind of smile that says, *Thank you, big sister, for coaching me through the debate and helping me get to this point.* It's the kind that says, *You thought I couldn't do it, but I did. What's your next move?*

When everyone is seated, I clear my throat, and the other five girls go quiet. I know I should probably make a speech or something, and I expect the right words to come to me like usual. I'm always calm and articulate in Committee meetings, safe and secure in the knowledge that I control everything that happens in this room. But having Abby here makes me jumpy, and the jumpiness makes me angry, and the anger leaves my mind completely blank, which makes me even angrier.

I take a deep breath like I taught Abby to do and pray everyone can't read my emotions all over my face. "I'd like to welcome our new representatives and congratulate them on their wins," I say, and then I decide that's enough of that. There's no reason for me to be like Vice Principal Rosenberg and make a huge deal about democracy.

"Thanks," Abby says. "It's so cool to be on this side of the table." She turns to Angelina. "Isn't it?"

Angelina glances at me for direction, and I congratulate myself on how effectively I got through to her. When I indicate that she can answer, she nods, but she doesn't speak. Abby's eyebrows scrunch together; she's clearly confused about why outgoing Angelina is suddenly acting so weird and withdrawn.

"You're gonna do great," Maya says.

"But not today," I clarify. "Abby and Angelina, you'll spend this Petition Day watching and listening so you can learn how we do things around here. At our next meeting, you'll be allowed to vote. Is that clear?"

"That's not fair," Abby says. "We're Committee members *now*. We got elected. Shouldn't we be allowed to—"

I ignore her. "Lily, go ahead and let the first petitioner in."

My sister falls silent, but it doesn't look like she's going to stay that way for long.

The first few requests are easy—maintenance for a jammed closet door and an appeal over a library fine incurred while the student was in the infirmary. A girl who hit me in the head with a volleyball last week in PE asks for permission to throw a birthday party in her dorm's lounge, and we deny it. The Chess Club president comes in and requests a space for their next few meetings, and we grant it. Abby and Angelina haven't said a word, and I start to relax. I'm certainly not convinced everything is going to be fine, but it's looking like *today* might be.

And then Abby's friend Grace comes in, and my sister's face lights up.

Grace slaps a budget request form down in front of me. "Hi," she says. "I'm here to petition to have the fall play reinstated."

I roll my eyes and slide the form toward her. "We've already voted on this. The play isn't happening."

"The argument you gave was that there wasn't enough money to hire an outside director," Grace says. I never told Grace that; Abby must've reported back to her. "I talked to Principal Winslow yesterday, and she said they posted the drama teacher position the day Ms. Gutierrez left. They've already started interviewing people, and they've narrowed it down to a few. So hiring an outside director won't be necessary."

"The money for the fall play has already been reallocated," I say. Sometimes petitioners back off when I use big words.

Grace doesn't even blink. "To where? That was a lot of money."

"It's not your concern where the money went," I say. "We split it up between several historically underfunded clubs. I'm sorry, but you'll have to wait until spring." I press the DENIED stamp down on her petition, and it makes a satisfying thump. "Please send in the next girl."

Abby and Grace lock eyes, and then my sister says, "I'd like to see this fall's budget information, please."

My heart speeds up the tiniest bit. "That's not relevant right now," I say. "You're supposed to be watching and learning about Petition Day. You can look at the budget when—"

Abby cuts me off, which no one else in this room would dare to do. "Seeing the budget would help Angelina and me learn. How are we supposed to know what 'not enough money' looks like if we haven't seen the numbers?"

"We're never going to get through Petition Day if we keep stopping to explain things to you," I say.

"Isn't that what we're supposed to be doing, though?" Lily asks. "Teaching them how the Committee works? I don't have any problem with showing them the budget spreadsheet."

"Me neither," says Maya.

"I have it right here," Gianna says, tapping her tablet. "I can send it now."

Abby smiles at me, sweet as the chocolate chip muffin in her hand. "Looks like you're outvoted, Syd," she says.

"That is *not* how the Committee votes," I snap, and it comes out higher and more hysterical than I intended. I have got to pull myself together.

"But this doesn't require a vote," says Maya. "They're Committee members; this is Committee information. They should have access to it."

I have never felt anything but total control here in this room, and even these tiny seeds of dissent give me vertigo, like I'm sitting on shifting sand instead of solid ground. But I tighten my grip on the reins and put my authoritative voice back on. Even

150

if I'm feeling off-balance, I have to make everyone believe I'm doing exactly what I want.

"Okay, you're right," I say. "Go ahead and send the budget spreadsheet to our new members, Gianna. I just didn't want to delay our petitioners. I'm sorry for taking up so much of your time, Grace."

"I don't mind," she says. "I'm happy to wait."

Gianna sends the spreadsheet, and Abby immediately opens it on her phone. When I don't object, Angelina tentatively takes out her own and does the same.

At first it's completely silent in the room, and for the briefest moment, I'm able to make myself believe that Abby and Angelina won't figure out where all the money for the play has gone. But it's not like these girls can't read a column of numbers, and after about twenty seconds, Abby's eyes widen. "Why does Astronomy Club have a seven-*thousand*-dollar budget?" she says. "Aren't there, like, two people in Astronomy Club?"

"There are six," I say. *And one of them is the coolest person in the entire school, and this is the only way she's ever going to like me.* "They petitioned to take a trip to Cape Canaveral to see the SpaceX Dragon launch. It's an expensive trip."

Abby's face is dark with anger and betrayal. "You took away our play so *six people* could go to Texas or wherever to see a *rocket*?"

"Cape Canaveral is in Florida," says Lily.

"Whatever! You know you can watch that stuff online,

151

right?" She looks around at the rest of the Committee. "You all agreed to this? Seriously?"

My Committee exchanges glances. I can tell they're all thinking the same thing—they *did* vote for this, and they're all implicated, regardless of how they actually feel about it. They're in too deep to dig themselves out now. Finally Maya says, "It's not fair that the same few clubs always get the most money. The play is really expensive, and—"

My sister cuts her off. "Yeah, yeah, I've heard it all before." She sighs. "I move that we vote on whether to cancel this ridiculous trip. And then I move that we vote on Grace's petition to reinstate the play."

"You're not a voting member today," I say. "You can't move that we do anything."

"Fine. I move that we vote on those things tomorrow."

"You can't—" I start, but it doesn't really matter either way. Everyone else will vote with me no matter when we do it. It'll be good for Abby to see that she's outnumbered.

Maybe by tomorrow I can scare my sister into submission too. She can't change any of our rulings by herself, but I don't want to deal with her stirring up trouble all year. I really, *really* hoped Abby would stay on my good side; I've tried my absolute hardest not to hurt her, and I don't want to do it now. But this Committee is all I have, and if she's going to try to ruin this for me, my first priority has to be protecting myself.

"Fine, we'll vote tomorrow," I say, and Abby looks up at me, surprised and a little suspicious. Lily, Gianna, and Maya look confused, but when I say, "All in favor?" and raise my hand, they put theirs up too and chorus, "Aye."

I find a Sharpie in my bag, cross out the DENIED stamp on Grace's petition, and stamp PENDING in the empty space beside it. It's the first time I've ever reversed one of my rulings, and even though I'm positive I can put everything back to how it should be tomorrow, it still feels awful.

There are no more unusual petitions today, but I'm off my game now, and Abby keeps asking questions, so getting through everyone takes absolutely forever. By the time we're done, the dinner bell is chiming, and I'm exhausted. I'm always tired after Petition Day, but in that good, accomplished way that comes from knowing I've given people exactly what they deserve. This time it's the kind of tired that makes me want to crawl into bed at seven o'clock and sleep for the rest of the week.

The rest of the girls pack up their things and sling their backpacks over their shoulders. "You coming to dinner, Sydney?" Lily asks, like she does every single Petition Day. It's a wonder she hasn't given up on me.

"Maybe in a little while," I say, though I know I can't handle the dining hall tonight.

Everyone says goodbye except Angelina, who still seems too scared to speak to me at all. Abby catches my eye on the way out and smiles. She looks ridiculously pleased with herself.

When everyone is gone, I lock the door, sit back down in my chair, and breathe deeply, reminding myself that every meeting won't be like this one. I will have total control over my Committee again. I really don't want to use the dirt I have on Abby, but I have more on her than I have on anyone else. If I just *threaten* to use it, things can go back to the way they used to be.

Capriana would never sit around and hope things worked themselves out, and I can't afford to do that either.

I go to the dining hall just long enough to make a sandwich, then eat it at my favorite desk in the library as I plan my next move. When I see girls leaving dinner and streaming back to their dorms, I pack up my stuff and head over to Stronger Hall. Abby opens the door as soon as I knock, a big smile on her face and light in her eyes, but her expression flattens when she sees me. "Oh," she says. "I thought you were Lydia."

"Well, I'm not," I say, and then I curse myself for sounding so defensive.

"Do you need something?" Abby asks.

Her door is still mostly closed, so I can't see into her room. "Is your roommate here?" I ask.

"Yeah." She opens the door wide enough for me to glimpse a girl with curly black hair sitting at her desk, then swings it shut again.

I don't really want to have this conversation in the middle of the hallway, but it's pretty empty right now; if I keep my voice low, it should be fine. "Come out here," I say.

My sister slips out the door, then closes it and leans against it, crossing her arms over her chest. Her face looks guarded, but her socks have pink whales on them, which pretty much counteracts the expression. "What's up?" she says. "I only have a minute."

"You need to stop pushing the Committee about the play," I say. "We've voted on it, it's over, and there's nothing you can do about it. Period. Okay?"

Abby's eyes narrow, and her chin lifts in that defiant tilt I'm starting to hate. "And what happens if I don't?"

I don't want to do this, but she's basically forcing me. "Listen, you've been doing really well here. You've been trying all kinds of new stuff and making lots of friends, and now you're becoming a leader. It's obvious everyone likes the new you. But I wonder how much they would respect you if they knew what you were like a few months ago? Those new friends of yours might be interested in what happened at our old school."

I expect Abby's eyes to widen like Angelina's did when I cornered her. I expect her to agree to do whatever I ask, like everyone else always does. But my sister's face doesn't change at all. "Are you seriously doing this right now?" she says. "Because it's not going to work."

Nobody's ever brushed me off like this before, and it takes effort not to show surprise. "I just think we could work together in a way that's beneficial to both of us," I say.

My sister sighs; it's almost as if she's bored with this conversation. "I don't have time for this," she says. "I have a history project due tomorrow. I need to go now."

She turns and puts her hand on the doorknob, and a flash of panic zips through me, which makes me furious. *She's* the one who should be afraid, not me.

"I'm not sure you understand what I'm telling you," I say. "If you don't back off—"

"No, I get what you're saying," Abby says. She's halfway into the room already. "Thanks for the heads-up. I'll see you first period. Bye, Syd."

The door closes behind her, and I hear the lock click into place. There's a burst of giggles from the other end of the hall, and even though those girls are much too far away to have heard us talking, I can't help feeling like it's directed at me.

I've had so many conversations like this since I joined the Committee, and not a single one of them has left me this unsettled.

Abby clearly understands what I was trying to tell her. I just get the sense that she doesn't care.

Chapter 16

It's very disconcerting to go into the next morning's Committee meeting with no idea what to expect. Now that Abby's had a whole night to think about her options, it's possible this will be the day she finally stops baiting me and starts following the rules. Or it could be the day I have to expose her for who she really is—or who she used to be, anyway—and bring everything she's built here at Brookside crashing to the ground. Considering the effort I've put into protecting her, it seems ridiculous that I'd be the one to unmask her.

Everything in me hopes I don't have to do it.

Abby arrives at the meeting a minute before the bell, hair in a neat side-braid, face completely untroubled. She says good morning to everyone and sits down directly across from me, which is not a good sign. But I force myself to look authoritative as I pull the small stack of pending petitions out of my backpack and slap them down on the table.

"Good morning," I say. "If everyone's ready, I'd like to start reviewing these petitions from—"

"I move that we discuss Grace's petition to reinstate the play," Abby says.

I swallow hard. I thought we'd dip our toes into this slowly; Grace's petition is at the bottom of the pile for a reason. I look my sister in the eyes, and she stares right back at me. I wish I hadn't taught her to embody a version of herself who isn't afraid.

Finally I say, "All right. Do you have something you'd like to say?"

Abby stands up, and even though that's not how we usually do things here, I have to admit that it lends her an extra air of authority. "There's not much to say about this that I didn't say yesterday," she says. "We don't need an outside director, so that argument for canceling the play doesn't hold up. It's true that the play is expensive, and of course other activities deserve funding too. But the budget indicates that all the money from the play *and* a portion of dance team and the soccer team has been given to Astronomy Club to fund their trip to Cape Canaveral, which is totally ridiculous. A trip like that benefits only a few people and hurts the rest of the Brookside community, unlike the play, which exists to entertain everyone. If Astronomy Club wants to take such an expensive trip, they should raise the money themselves."

Until this moment, I had no idea it was possible to be so proud of someone and so furious with her at the same time.

And then Abby continues, "Last night I talked to Charlotte, who runs the dance team, and Macy, the captain of the soccer team. Charlotte told me that Sydney hates her because she beat her in a science trivia competition last year—it's been nearly impossible for her to get petitions approved, as I'm sure you all know. Macy told me that she got the single room Syd wanted in the housing lottery, which means Sydney has to live with two girls she doesn't like. And she clearly has a personal grudge against me because she wants to be the only successful Carrington at Brookside. It killed her when I got a role in the play, which showed her I could be successful too. And now here I am on the Committee, showing her up again. So of course she doesn't want to give me or my friends what we want."

All that pride melts away like a candle held up to a blow-torch. I can feel my cheeks going pink, and I desperately struggle for control; I'm pretty sure I've never blushed in front of my Committee before, and this is *not* the time to start.

"So in conclusion," Abby says, "I don't think the decision to cancel the play has anything to do with money or fairness. I think you all know that. But now that I'm on the Committee, we're actually going to do something about it. I'm going to keep bringing this up every day until the play gets reinstated. I don't care if I drive you all crazy."

My sister sits down, and the rest of the Committee blinks at her in shock.

"Abby," I say, as calm and quiet as I can manage, "do you remember what I said last night?"

She holds my gaze steadily. "You mean when you threatened to blackmail me?"

Nobody has ever outright accused me of blackmail before. I have no idea what to do, so I just say, "Um."

"See, it's funny," Abby says. "Up until last week, that really would've scared me. The old me would've been totally terrified that if anyone knew my secrets, nobody would like me. But then *you* told me that I had to own my failures and my successes, because they're all parts of me. You told me it's obvious everyone likes who I am now. And you know what? I think that's actually true."

"You really don't want to—" I start, but my sister turns to the rest of the Committee and talks right over me.

"Sydney warned me last night that if I didn't stop fighting for the play, she'd tell everyone about something embarrassing that happened at our old school. But the thing is, I don't care anymore if you guys know what happened. It's over, and embarrassing stuff in our pasts doesn't have to affect us forever, right?"

For years, I've wished Abby could move past what happened at the talent show, that she could find a way to not let it affect her. And now that she's finally doing it, all I want is for her to turn back into the scared little girl she used to be. I cross my arms tight over my stomach, afraid I might be sick if I don't physically hold myself together.

"Here's what happened," Abby says. "In third grade, I

160

entered the school talent show. I was going to sing 'Castle on a Cloud' from *Les Mis*—I was so obsessed with that song. So I got up onstage in front of the entire school, and my music started, and I just . . . couldn't make myself sing. I was totally frozen. And then I looked out at the audience, and I saw hundreds of kids staring at me, and I totally freaked out and started crying. It was *super* embarrassing. My nose was dripping all over the place, and a teacher had to come get me off the stage. After that, kids started teasing me and making these stupid 'boo-hoo' noises whenever I got up in front of the class, and it got to the point where I wouldn't give presentations or even raise my hand because I was scared of how people would react. I even stopped going on class trips and stuff because I was afraid of being teased. I missed out on so much.

"But here's the thing: When I came to Brookside, none of those people were around anymore, and nobody here knew me, and I decided things were going to be different—or that *I* was going to be different, I guess. And then . . . I just *was*. That scared girl isn't who I am anymore. Am I still embarrassed about what happened? Yeah. Of course. It's always going to be embarrassing to think about. But it's not going to stop me from doing anything else I want to do. I bet you guys don't respect me less because you know that story, right?"

Angelina's looking up at my sister, wide-eyed with awe. She shakes her head.

"Definitely not," Lily agrees. "At least you got up there and tried. I once signed up for the talent show at my old school, but I changed my mind five minutes before and hid in the bathroom for like an hour."

Abby smiles. "Thanks, you guys. It's kind of a relief to tell that story, honestly."

I've lost every ounce of control I had over my sister.

"I've only been on this Committee for two days, and I don't know what happened before I got here," Abby continues. "But I have this feeling that Sydney knows some embarrassing stuff about the rest of you too. I bet she's tried to make you think she's protecting you by keeping those things secret. But she's not. She's just controlling you. Think of what it would feel like to not be afraid of her. You could actually say what you think, vote how you want. That's why you ran for the Committee, right?"

She pauses to let that sink in, meeting each girl's eyes in turn. Some of them look down at the table.

Some of them don't.

"Abby, *please* . . ." I say, but she ignores me.

"I move that we vote on Grace's petition to reinstate the play," she says again, and I get that swooping feeling in my chest that happens when you miss a step on a staircase and your body's positive, just for a second, that it's going to plummet into oblivion.

"Fine," I say, forcing my voice not to tremble. Even if Abby's motivational speech has gotten through to the other girls, I tell myself there's no way they'll change their minds about voting against me. Angelina's too scared, and the other girls will need to weigh their options very carefully. The fact that we're all in this together means they won't be able to wriggle out from under my influence as easily as Abby.

Right?

"All in favor of reinstating the play?" I say.

"Aye," Abby says loudly, like she's trying to project to the back of a theater. She raises her hand high. Then she turns to Angelina, eyes wide and expectant.

And to my utter horror, Angelina's hand slowly creeps into the air. "Aye," she says, so quietly it's almost a whisper.

I skewer her with my gaze. "Angelina," I warn.

"Whatever she knows, it's not a big deal," Abby says. "You can tell us, and then she won't have any power over you. We're still going to like you no matter what it is."

"No influencing the vote," I say. That's not an actual rule, but I'm grasping at straws. I've never needed it to be an actual rule before.

Angelina takes a deep breath. "I wrote this really stupid, gushy letter to a guy in my youth group last year," she says. "This girl took a picture of it and sent it to everyone. I'm pretty sure he saw it too. I had to drop out of youth group for a while." She tips her head toward me. "She has a copy of it somehow."

"Oh god, I know that feeling," Gianna says. "I wrote a letter to a boy in my class when I was in fifth grade, and he *dropped it* in the cafeteria, and everyone saw it. They made so much fun of me."

"But it doesn't matter now, right?" Abby says, her voice soothing. "Even if people find out, it's ancient history."

"I'm glad you told us," Lily says to Angelina. "That was brave."

"And now you can express your real opinions without having to worry," says Abby.

Angelina looks up, a triumphant smile tugging at the corners of her mouth. "Yeah, I can," she says. And when she looks at me, her face says, *I can do anything I want now.* Frankly it's kind of terrifying. I barely know Angelina; I have no idea what she's capable of doing.

But I tell myself this is fine. If the sixth graders want to rebel, let them. We still outnumber them two to one. It's not ideal, but every vote will still go my way.

And then Lily takes a deep breath.

"I write fan fiction about my favorite series of books and post them online," she says. Her cheeks are bright pink, but her voice is strong and clear. "Some of them are, um . . . romances. With girls and dragons."

"Wow, really?" Maya says. "That sounds awesome. I love fanfic."

"Me too," says Angelina.

"Sydney found my screen name and threatened to spread it around and tell everyone it's me in the stories, that I'm in love with a fictional dragon," Lily continues. "Which I'm *obviously* not. I just really, *really* like these books. And Brandozer is my favorite character."

"What's the series?" asks Abby.

"The Chronicles of Wings and Teeth," Lily says. She digs a book out of her bag and holds it up—it's got a giant yellow dragon plummeting through a storm on the front. "This is book eleven, but I have the others if you ever want to borrow one."

"I'd love to," Abby says. "Thanks. Can I read your fanfic too, after I know the characters?"

"Yeah, I guess, if you want to," Lily says. "My stories are, um . . . Well, they're actually pretty popular."

"That's amazing," Abby says. "You shouldn't ever let anyone make you feel ashamed of the stuff you love."

Lily's sitting up straight now, and it's only then that I realize I'm used to seeing her hunched over. There's something else new about her too: a flash of anger in her eyes. I really, *really* can't afford for anyone else to get angry.

And then she looks right at me and says, "I vote to reinstate the play."

My stomach feels like it has dropped out of my body. Part of me is afraid that if I look down, it'll be sitting there on the gray industrial carpet. I desperately want to rub my left eye—it gets super dry when I'm nervous—but I lace my fingers tightly together and force them to stay folded in my lap.

"That's three votes for reinstating the play," Abby says. "Anyone else in favor? Maya? Gianna? We only need one of you."

Both girls look at me, then back down at the table, and a tiny pinprick of hope shines through the fog of fear clouding my brain. The dirt I had on Abby and Lily and Angelina was embarrassing, but nothing they've done is against the rules. The stuff I have on Gianna and Maya could actually get them in trouble.

If they vote for the play, I can have them sent straight to Principal Winslow's office.

"I know she has something on you," Abby presses. "You'll feel so much better if you get it off your chest. I promise."

Gianna shakes her head. "I, um . . . I agree with Sydney's arguments."

"Me too," says Maya. Neither of them sounds sincere, but it doesn't matter. I don't need them to be honest. I just need them to be loyal.

"Well, okay," Abby says, though she sounds a little defeated. "All against?"

I put my hand in the air and say, "Nay," and Gianna and Maya echo me. My stomach settles back into place.

"Okay," Abby says. "Three for and three against. What happens now?"

"I don't know," Lily says. "We've never had this problem before."

"I'll look it up." Gianna starts tapping at her tablet.

And then I realize exactly what will happen now, and it's like someone has shot a bolt of lightning up my spine. I was so focused on maintaining control of *some* of my Committee that I lost sight of the big picture. Dealing with the consequences of a tie might actually be worse than a loss. I am the worst strategist of all time. If Capriana the Rogue had run her life like I'm running mine today, she would've ended up dead in a ditch by the end of her first campaign.

"Here it is," Gianna says. "'In the event of a tie, the

Committee's faculty advisor will cast the deciding vote. She should be provided with all relevant information so she can make an informed decision.'"

My carefully calibrated, totally unfair budget is about to land in Vice Principal Rosenberg's hands.

Chapter 17

The rest of the day goes by in a haze. I don't remember sitting through my classes, doing my homework, or eating dinner, though I'm pretty sure my body goes through the motions. I get in bed at the regular time, put on my headphones, and watch Mars rover videos I've seen a million times to lull me to sleep. But long after Olivia and Hannah have gone quiet in their bedroom, I'm still awake.

I still haven't slept by the time they get up and leave for field hockey practice in the morning.

Lying here and stewing in anxiety isn't doing me any good, so I put on my uniform and my Capriana boots and head across the quad to the Student Center an hour early. I'm vaguely hungry, but I can't face the dining hall, so I figure I'll get some peanut butter crackers from the vending machine. Once I'm standing in front of the glowing glass, though, the thought of eating makes me nauseated. I slink into the Student Government Office instead, lock the door behind me, and lie down under the table, my backpack tucked under my head. Decades of students have stuck chewed gum and scratched their initials on the underside, and in one corner, someone has written NOPE in blue Sharpie. I don't know who that girl was, but I know exactly how she felt.

When the ten-minute bell rings, I get up, smooth my skirt, and unlock the door. I sit down at the head of the table in my special chair, hands folded in front of me, and wait. I've gotten good at swallowing my emotions down, and I won't give anyone the satisfaction of letting them show today.

The rest of the Committee trickles in, and everyone says hi to me like usual, but today nobody looks directly at me. I'm used to people avoiding my gaze because they're scared, but this feels like they're looking away from a wounded animal out of pity. It's the same exact way Josh and Dev and Antonia looked at me when they kicked me out of the D&D group.

Vice Principal Rosenberg breezes in as the bell rings, dressed in a red pantsuit and smiling her face off. Even the way her gray-blond ponytail swings is enthusiastic. She sits down across the table from me, looking totally at home already. "Good morning, young women!" she says. "I'm so delighted to do my sworn duty and take part in your democratic process today. This is just like Congress—did you know that when there's a tied vote in the Senate, the Vice President is called upon to break it?"

Lily nods. "We learned about that in social studies."

"Well, then, I'm glad our faculty is doing such a great job of educating young minds." Vice Principal Rosenberg beams at us. "So! What am I voting on today? Who would like to present the facts?" She looks at me, but when Abby leaps to her feet instead, she literally claps with delight. "One of our new members taking such initiative already! Well done, Abbi. Lay it all out for me."

Abby pulls Grace's petition and a printed copy of the budget out of her backpack and slides them across the table. I expect her to launch into the same speech she gave the Committee yesterday about how I try to manipulate people with information, but instead she sticks to the facts about how the Committee canceled the play and gave the money to another club in a way she feels is unfair. When she points out the part of the spreadsheet where Astronomy Club's budget is listed, the shock and dismay that crosses our vice principal's face makes my stomach twist into a knot. I'm suddenly glad I wasn't able to eat.

"Seven *thousand* dollars?" Vice Principal Rosenberg asks. "Is this a typo?"

"No," Abby says.

"What can this *possibly* be for?"

Abby looks at me, and I clear my throat and sit up as straight as I can. "Astronomy Club petitioned to take a trip to Cape Canaveral to see a rocket launch," I say. "It's a really cool educational opportunity. They found someone willing to give them a private tour of mission control. So the budget covers the fee for that, plane tickets, rental cars, food, and lodgings for six girls and two chaperones for three days and two nights—"

"Plus, we bought them a new telescope," Gianna chimes in. "That was a different petition."

"It was a great tool for learning," I say. "When else are those girls going to see the rings of Saturn? When are they going to see a rocket launch in person? A lot of them are interested in going into STEM fields, and we can help them pursue those dreams." I picture Jenna as a grown-up, sitting in front of an array of consoles and helping to land the first humans on Mars. As she skillfully navigates the astronauts down through the red dust, maybe she'll think about the girl who gave her the start she needed way back in eighth grade.

"I knew about the trip, but this is . . ." Vice Principal Rosenberg shakes her head like she's trying to clear it. "I thought Astronomy Club had been doing its own fundraising. And I thought the girls' parents were chipping in. Where did all this money even come from? The play didn't have a seven-thousand-dollar budget."

"Some of it came from here," Abby says, pointing at the dance team line on the spreadsheet. "And the soccer team was supposed to get new uniforms this year, which isn't happening now. I'm not sure where else. But I think all the clubs and teams that were unfairly robbed deserve their funding back."

Vice Principal Rosenberg takes off her reading glasses and rubs her eyes, then looks around the room. "You all voted for this reallocation of funds?"

"Yes, they all did," I say before anyone else can speak.

"Well, not Angelina and me," Abby says. "We weren't elected yet."

Vice Principal Rosenberg sighs heavily and looks at the seventh and eighth graders. "I'm really disappointed in you all. Obviously I'm in favor of supporting girls who want to go into STEM fields, but Brookside's arts and athletics programs are important too. No group should ever lose *all* their opportunities at the expense of giving something extravagant to another. I would've thought that was obvious." And then she looks straight at me. "Is *this* why you've been keeping me away from meetings all this time?"

An unexpected wave of shame sweeps over me. I've never known how to make my fellow students like me, but I've always, *always* been in good standing with the adults. It's been years since I've heard anything but *Excellent work, Sydney* and *What a bright future you have*. I can't even remember the last time a teacher said she was disappointed in me. I don't think it's ever happened before.

"I . . . No," I say, but I can feel my face turning red. I think about apologizing, but that would indicate that I think I'm wrong, and I can't make myself do it. "We thought what we did was the best option," I finish lamely.

"Do the rest of you have anything you'd like to say for yourselves before I vote?" Vice Principal Rosenberg asks.

I shake my head. Gianna and Maya do the same.

"I regret my initial vote to cancel the play," Lily says. "Not that it makes any difference, since I would've been outvoted anyway. But I realize now that what we did was wrong."

"Thank you, Lily," says Vice Principal Rosenberg. "All right. I cast my vote in favor of reinstating the play. All the funds that were originally allocated to it must be returned. We extended an offer to a new drama teacher this morning, and she accepted the job, so she will take over as director, and everything will proceed as originally planned."

The sunniest smile I've ever seen breaks across my sister's face. *"Thank you,"* she breathes. "Oh my god, thank you so much, seriously."

It was obvious this was coming, and I don't mind so much that the play has been reinstated. My sister got what makes her happiest, and I never had to show weakness by backing down. But when I think about telling Jenna that we have to pull the funding for Astronomy Club's trip, my heart melts like a sad scoop of ice cream someone dropped on the sidewalk. She probably won't get angry, but she'll be so disappointed, and that's almost worse. I'm pretty sure she only ever talked to me because she knew I had the power to give her things she wanted. Now that I have to take them away, I won't be "the best" anymore. I won't be anything at all. She won't even notice I exist.

"Okay," I say, and my voice comes out weirdly breathy. "The, um . . . The motion passes." I scramble to get my stamps and ink pad—apparently I've forgotten to take them out of my back-pack. When I finally find the APPROVED stamp, I hold it up and reach across the table for Grace's petition. "Can I, um . . ."

But Vice Principal Rosenberg doesn't give it to me. "Furthermore," she says, "as your faculty advisor, I feel it's my duty to suspend this Committee, effective immediately. I'll bring this case to the board of directors for further review. I need you to send me documentation of all the petitions you have approved and rejected so far this school year and a copy of the budget, please."

I blink at her. "But . . . we . . ."

"You're shutting down the Committee?" Maya asks. I'm sure the look of complete horror on her face mirrors mine exactly.

"Hopefully it won't be permanent. But as things stand, you girls are not governing the student body in a fair and unbiased manner. Some big changes clearly need to be made."

"But Angelina and I were just elected," Abby says. "We've only been here two days. *We* shouldn't be punished when we haven't done anything wrong."

"I'm not trying to punish you," Vice Principal Rosenberg says. "Honestly I blame myself for what happened here. When Sydney told me this Committee should be a safe space for students to work without adult input, I bought into that. Even when students came to me to complain that things weren't operating entirely fairly in here, I thought they were just upset that their specific petitions hadn't been approved. I assumed you girls were mature enough to make decisions that were right for our whole community, and I clearly shouldn't have. I know you're trying, but you're so young, and . . . Well, people need guidance as they learn to be good leaders. I should've been supervising you much more closely."

My mind is spinning now, desperately scrambling for a way I can fix this. "We can, um, put some new protocols in place,"

I offer. "We could work out a system of reporting back to you. Like maybe a weekly meeting or something? You could come in every Friday, and we could tell you what we've been up to." I wouldn't have to tell her *everything*. And even if Abby isn't afraid of me anymore, I could probably dig up more dirt on Lily or Angelina, something they really *would* be embarrassed for all their classmates to know. I wouldn't even need to convince both of them to vote with me. A four-to-two vote is still a win.

But Vice Principal Rosenberg says, "I think we're going to need more accountability than that. If the board chooses to keep the Committee running at all, I think an adult needs to be present at every meeting. Maybe me, maybe someone else. There's a lot to think about."

I feel like someone has stepped right on my melted-ice-cream heart with a giant, dirty boot.

Vice Principal Rosenberg stands up. "Until further notice, I'm adding all of you to Ms. Khaled's first-period study hall. There's a board meeting tomorrow, and I'll put this on the agenda."

Nobody speaks, and I wonder if every girl feels the same flood of despair that I'm feeling, filling up her chest and drowning her words. Finally Lily manages to say, "Okay."

"I'll be in touch soon," our vice principal says in a formal, tired voice, the complete opposite of the bouncy enthusiasm she came in with.

And then she's gone, and so is everything I've worked for since I arrived at Brookside.

✗ ✗ ✗

Chapter 18

When the bell rings, I go straight to the infirmary and tell Nurse Richie I have a stomachache, and she writes me a pass to get out of classes. I head back to my room, climb into bed in my uniform, pull the covers over my head, and stay there the rest of the day. When a campus-wide email arrives stating that Petition Day is suspended until further notice and that girls should contact Vice Principal Rosenberg directly with any issues or requests, I turn off my phone and toss it onto the floor. I'm sure nobody will try to contact me. Even when I had power, nobody ever did.

I run out of granola bars by the next morning, and hunger finally forces me out of my room. When I reach the dining hall, my mouth drops open. The walls are covered in posters as bright and glittery as the campaign posters that came down a few days ago.

SAVE THE COMMITTEE!

WE DESERVE A VOICE!

**GOVERNMENT BY THE STUDENTS,
FOR THE STUDENTS!**

For the first time in a day and a half, I feel a swell of hope. People have rushed to our defense—*my* defense, really, since I'm the only one who has ever really made a Committee decision. Sure, my choices haven't always been 100 percent fair, but people obviously still like being governed by me. This is proof, and the administration will have to listen. Maybe Vice Principal Rosenberg wanted to overrule us, but there's no way she'll overrule the entire student body. She's too much of a sucker for democracy.

And then I notice some of the other posters.

PRESIDENT OR BLACKMAILER?

DOWN WITH DICTATOR CARRINGTON!

IMPEACH SYDNEY!

I realize then that everyone knows *everything* that happened in our last few meetings. The rest of the Committee girls must've told their friends, who told *their* friends. News spreads so fast around here. Even the administration must know everything by now.

I wonder who made those signs. I wonder if it was Abby.

Everything in me wants to turn around and run, but I forbid myself to back down at the first signs of aggression. That's what Gianna and Maya do, and even though it's what I want from them, it doesn't make me *respect* them. So I hold my head high as I go through the serving line and pile my plate high with eggs and toast and bacon. It smells way better than usual, which I guess is what happens when you eat almost nothing for an entire day. I get my juice from the dispenser and look around for a place to sit.

There are several spots open at the table where Dance Team Charlotte is sitting, but I have no desire to deal with her today. There's also a spot next to Lily, whose nose is buried in her dragon book of the day, but I don't want to face her either—for all I know, *she* made the posters. The Astronomy Club girls are clustered by the window, and the chair across from Jenna is empty. But if I sit there, she'll start talking about how excited she is for the Cape Canaveral trip, and then I'll have to tell her that the funding has been pulled, and . . . I can't. I'm not ready to disappoint her like that.

I head toward a table of seventh graders I don't really know, and when one of them sees me coming, she widens her eyes and then looks away, just like usual. Maybe the anti-Sydney signs haven't made any difference and I still have the status I always had. But then the girl leans over and whispers something to her friend. Both of them glance at me, glance at the signs . . . and *laugh*.

Nobody at Brookside has ever dared to laugh at me.

I slam my tray down on the nearest table so hard my juice tips over, splashing another girl. I don't even pause to apologize before I'm running toward the double doors. I know it's not dignified and that I'm probably drawing even more unwanted attention to myself, but my chest is tightening, and my face feels hot, and I can't be in that dining hall full of judgmental eyes for one more second. This must be exactly how Abby used to feel.

I sprint across the lawn, and I don't stop running until I reach my safe haven, the library. When I burst through the doors, panting, Ms. Stamos looks up from her desk. "Sydney? Are you okay?"

I nod, but I don't stop walking until I'm at my favorite desk in the back of the room, and that's where the tears that have been threatening for a whole day finally spill over. I don't bother to wipe them away. I'm right by the window, and if anyone in the quad bothered to look up, they'd probably see me crying, but it doesn't matter anymore. If everyone knows the truth about me already, what's the point of keeping up my strong facade? My reputation is already in shambles.

And then I hear footsteps behind me, soft on the carpet. My sister's voice says, "Syd?"

I swipe my hands angrily over my cheeks and turn around. "What are you doing here?"

"I saw you run out of the dining hall. I wanted to make sure you were okay." She takes a tentative step toward me, like I'm a feral cat who might bite her. "Are you? Okay?"

Ordinarily I would tell her to leave me alone, that I don't want to talk about it—it's what I've been telling my family for years. It's what I said in sixth grade when I overheard the other kids in my history group making fun of the enthusiastic way I raised my hand in class. It's what I said after Josh and Dev and Antonia told me I wasn't invited back to the D&D group, that the selfish way I was playing was ruining the game for everyone. Talking about your emotions just forces you to feel them more and makes you look weak.

But for some reason, I can't bring myself to put up a strong front right now.

"I don't know," I say.

Abby takes that as an invitation and approaches, leaning against the side of the desk. She's still not quite close enough to touch me. "What happened?" she asks.

"You know what happened," I snap. "You were there."

"Are you, um . . . Is it the posters?"

"It's just . . . *everything*." A few more tears spill down my cheeks. "But yeah, the giant posters calling me a dictator and a blackmailer didn't help. You didn't make those, did you?"

"*No*," Abby says. "I would never. I don't want you off the Committee. I just want things to be fair."

If I were her, I would definitely want me off the Committee. She's a much better person than I am.

"Do you know who did make them?" I ask.

"I think it was Angelina's friends. The ones who ran her campaign. She told them you blackmailed her, and they were pretty pissed. But nobody's really going to impeach you, right? Is that even a thing?"

I wrap my arms tight around myself; it's not cold in the library, but I feel weirdly shivery. "The board could remove me," I say. "Or the administration could. They probably will. I bet Vice Principal Rosenberg knows everything by now. About the, um . . . the way I manipulated people."

"It doesn't seem like she'd remove you without letting the students vote on it, though. Maybe all you have to do is apologize and say you'll run things more fairly, and people will forgive you."

I shake my head. "Nobody's going to forgive me."

"You're a good leader," Abby insists. "I've seen you at Petition Day. And people obviously like you or they wouldn't have elected you."

"They didn't elect me because they *like* me," I say. "I gamed the system." I've always been proud of how I pulled it off, but now my voice comes out sounding bitter.

"Oh." Abby blinks at me for a second, but then she rallies. "Well, I bet your friends would help you run a campaign, like Grace did for me. You know, help people see that you're truly sorry for what you did?"

I snort. "What friends?"

"You have tons of friends. Every time I see you in the dining hall, you're sitting at tables full of people who are laughing at your jokes."

"People only laugh at my jokes because they're afraid of me. *Everyone's* afraid of me. Or they were before today, anyway."

Abby looks confused. "Why? You're not that scary."

"Because I wanted them to be. Because I'm in charge of whether they get the things they want. If you want money for your club or an off-campus pass, are you seriously going to tell the president of the Committee that she can't sit with you? But if I don't have the Committee, then I don't have . . . Well. Anything."

My sister blinks at me. "Oh," she says.

"Or, um. Any*one*." I swallow hard. "I know you can't understand this because everyone loves you, but I don't have friends. Not *any*."

"I do understand," Abby says quietly. "I haven't either the last couple of years."

We're both quiet for a minute. It's starting to rain, and we look out the window at the bright umbrellas bobbing across the hazy gray-green of the quad. Finally I say, "That's why I canceled the play, you know."

Abby turns to look at me again, and there's a little crease between her eyebrows that makes her look exactly like our mom. "Because . . . people were afraid of you?"

"Because I wanted you to have friends."

"What does that have to do with the play?"

"I was trying to protect you," I say. "You were doing so well here, and you were hanging out with all these new people, and . . . I didn't want you in another situation where everything could fall apart. I didn't want you to get teased again."

"You canceled the play because you wanted to *protect me*?"

It sounds ridiculous when she puts it that way, but I nod. "I tried to stop you from auditioning, but you wouldn't listen. So . . . I don't know. I wanted Brookside to be different for you. I wanted you to have lots of opportunities to make up for all the ones you've missed."

Understanding dawns on my sister's face. "That's why you helped me with the debate even though you didn't want me to win." I nod. "Syd, that's . . ." She swallows hard. "I thought you just didn't want me to be happy. Because you were jealous or something."

"No, I . . . No. I'm the big sister. I'm supposed to protect you. I had to do something before you failed again."

"But that's what I still don't get," Abby says. "The audition went well, and then the debate was good too—you saw. I didn't need protecting. And even after that, you still tried to keep the play from happening."

"I'm sorry," I say. "I really am. I wanted to give it back. But it would've made me look weak if I'd backed down." I pick at my nail. "Plus, it *was* really expensive."

"But you still gave *seven thousand dollars* to Astronomy Club. I had to fight to get you to give three hundred dollars to Art Club. Are you even *in* Astronomy Club?"

I shake my head, and horrifyingly another tear sneaks out from under my glasses.

Abby's face softens. "Why not? You love astronomy. Remember how obsessed you were with the Mars rover? And how excited you were when Dad took you to see that meteor shower?"

"It doesn't matter," I say. "They wouldn't want me. Especially now that I have to cancel their trip. They're going to hate me."

"I'm sure they'll understand," Abby says. "If you're really worried, tell them it's Vice Principal Rosenberg's fault. Is the girl who runs it really mean or something?"

"*No*," I say. "Jenna's *so* nice. She's the first person who ever talked to me at Brookside."

Abby smiles. "See? You do have a friend!"

"She's not my friend. We've never even hung out."

"Okay, but you could, right? If you like her?"

"I don't know." I sniffle hard and dig through my bag until I find a balled-up dining hall napkin to wipe my nose. "What if she's only nice to me because I run Petition Day? And she knows I can get stuff for her club? That's why everyone else is nice to me."

"But you said she talked to you on your first day. And you didn't have any power then."

"Yeah, but I was so awkward with her. And it's not like she ever tried very hard to be my friend."

"I mean, if you were trying to scare everyone all the time, maybe you weren't super friendly either?"

I want to argue with Abby, but she's actually not wrong.

The five-minute bell rings, and my sister stands up. "Anyway, I bet she'd let you join her club. You should talk to her. Do you want me to go with you? After class this afternoon?"

I can't remember the last time someone offered to help me. I can't remember the last time I asked.

I nod. And then I burst into tears again.

"Oh no, it's okay," Abby says, and then she launches herself forward and hugs me. She's standing and I'm sitting, so it's mostly just an awkward tangle of limbs, and the buttons on the sleeve of her blazer catch on my hair, but it's kind of nice anyway. I don't think we've hugged since I left for Brookside at the beginning of last year.

"Why are you crying now?" she says. "It's going to work out. I promise."

"I don't even . . ." I bury my face in the shoulder of her blazer. "I'm just so *hungry.*"

She laughs and lets go of me. "Well, *that's* easy to fix. Come on, I bet Ms. Stamos will write us a pass, and we'll go get you a bagel. Sesame, toasted, not too much cream cheese. Okay?"

I nod. A bagel sounds like the most glorious thing in the world right now.

The second-best thing is that my sister remembers exactly what kind of bagels I like. I've kept her at a distance for so long, but she never stopped paying attention.

Abby picks up her bag and heads toward the door, assuming I'll follow, but I just sit there staring at her. It's so hard to believe how different she is now than she was on the drive up to Brookside a month ago. It seems impossible that this strong, confident version of my sister has been hiding inside her all this time.

Abby looks back over her shoulder and sees me staring. "Are you coming? Why are you looking at me weird?"

I wish I could tell her how proud of her I am, how much

I appreciate what she's doing for me. But I've never been great at that kind of thing, so I just say, "I really like your hair like that."

She smiles with all her teeth. "Thank you," she says.

I think maybe she knows what I mean.

Chapter 19

SYDNEY

Vice Principal Rosenberg calls me into her office at lunch. I perch on the very edge of the hard wooden chair across from her desk, heart pounding in my ears, as she breaks the news that because I irresponsibly allocated funds, canceled student activities without permission, and bullied my fellow Committee members, I am no longer allowed to serve as eighth-grade representative. Once the school board decides on the best way for the Committee to function in the future, Lily will take over as president, and a special election will be held for a new eighth grader to replace me. After just six short weeks, every ounce of power I've earned is slipping right through my fingers.

"I met with the remaining Committee members this morning," Vice Principal Rosenberg continues. "I asked for their help working out an appropriate punishment for you. Ordinarily you'd be suspended for mishandling school funds and manipu-lating students, but the other girls said they're willing to let you off without suspension if you spend the rest of this year doing community service for the clubs whose budgets you tried to cut. You'd be painting flats for the fall and spring plays, washing uniforms for our athletes after their meets and practices, and doing whatever other grunt work they decide to give you. Does that sound fair?"

Letting Grace and Charlotte and Macy boss me around for the rest of eighth grade sounds pretty awful, especially when I'm used to being the one in control. Things won't even get better once the school year is over; when Mom and Dad find out about what's been going on, they'll ground me for the entire summer. But if I'm honest with myself, I'm probably getting off easy. At least when I apply to high schools, my record will be clean.

"Yeah, that's probably fair," I say. My left eye is so dry it's stinging, and I rub it under my glasses. "Um, I know it's prob-ably too late for this, but . . . I wanted to say I'm sorry. I never meant to hurt anyone. Things just got a little out of control."

Vice Principal Rosenberg looks at me over her glasses, one eyebrow raised. "'A little out of control' seems like a bit of an understatement, but I'm glad to hear you say that. I think it would hold more weight if you apologized to the rest of the Committee, though."

I nod. "I'll tell them." That'll be hard, but it's the right thing to do, especially when they've been lenient with me.

Vice Principal Rosenberg and I sit in silence for a minute, and

I know I should feel devastated. I've lost absolutely everything I've been working for. But weirdly enough, the feeling that settles over me is mostly one of calm. For the first time since I got to Brookside, I have nothing to hide. For the last year, I've constantly felt as if I were juggling twenty plates. Part of me wishes I hadn't dropped them all, of course. But now that they're in shards at my feet, another part of me is relieved that they're gone. I'm being offered an unexpected opportunity to start over.

"Do you have any questions?" Vice Principal Rosenberg asks.

I shake my head. Everything seems pretty clear right now.

"Then I think that's all for the moment," she says. "I'll talk to the heads of the clubs you'll be serving, and we'll work out a schedule for you. Until then, you're free to go."

And when I stand up to leave, I actually *do* feel free.

• • •

When I arrive to meet Abby after her last class, she's sitting on the steps outside and talking to a girl with a heart-shaped face and curly hair. As I approach, she says something that makes the other girl laugh, and they lean together like they've known each other for years and not just a few weeks. "Hey!" she calls when she spots me. "Syd, come meet my roommate. This is Christina. And this is my big sister."

"Hi," I say. When Abby stares at me like I'm supposed to do something else, I add, "Nice to meet you. I'm Sydney."

"I, um . . . I know who you are," Christina says. Her voice is breathy, and her cheeks flush the second the words are out of her mouth. "I mean . . . Nice to meet you too?" Her eyes dart back to Abby. "I, um, I have tennis. I gotta go. See you at dinner?"

"See you," Abby says, and Christina bolts. Abby doesn't seem to think it's weird, though, so maybe it's not because of me. "Ready for our secret mission?"

I'm not ready at all. Since this morning, every time I've thought about talking to Jenna, my heart has done this weird spinning-leaping thing, like it's trying to twist free and escape. And since I've been thinking about it approximately every six seconds, I'm exhausted with the effort of holding myself together. What if she's furious that we have to cancel the trip and throws me out of her room? What if she just doesn't want me in her club? What if she slams the door in my face before I can say anything at all? What if she's perfectly nice about the whole thing but I act so awkward or standoffish or overeager that I still manage to ruin everything anyway?

I tell myself I have nothing else to lose. The worst thing that can possibly happen is that I'm not friends with Jenna when the conversation ends, and since I'm not friends with her now, I won't be any worse off. But right now I can cling to a shred of possibility that if I get my act together, she might really like me. Once I confront the problem head-on and know the outcome, that fragile slip of hope will disappear.

"Sydney?" Abby says.

My sister will be with me the whole time. She's great at making friends. Even if I'm a disaster, maybe Abby will say the right thing and save me. It's weird to be able to count on her for something like this.

"Yeah," I say. "I'm ready."

We walk across campus toward Jenna's dorm. Abby doesn't speak; it's almost like she can tell I'm practicing what to say in my head and doesn't want to interrupt. We unconsciously time our steps to each other's, and it reminds me of the way we used to link arms and try to skip when we were little kids. We could never get the rhythm right; Abby was always headed up to the top of her bounce as I was coming down, and it meant neither of us got to go as high. It's not like I'd ever skip in public, but I bet we could do it correctly now if we tried, each of us pulling the other one higher.

Too soon, Abby's swiping her ID and holding the door of Jenna's dorm for me. "Do you know which room she's in?" she asks.

I do know—I looked it up in the student directory once—but it seems creepy to say that, so I shake my head. "That's okay," Abby says, and she marches right up to a group of girls in the lobby. "Excuse me, do you know which room Jenna—What's her last name, Syd?"

"Jenna Aristide," I say, and for some reason I blush.

"Right. Do you know where she lives?"

"I think she's in 221," says one of the girls.

"Thanks," says Abby, and when I don't move, she tugs on my arm. "Come on!"

I snatch my arm away. "Okay, god, I'm coming." Then I

realize I've used my Mean Sydney voice, the one that has always been my armor. Abby doesn't even look surprised, which means I've probably used it on her a lot, and that makes me feel even worse. "Sorry," I say. "I'm just—"

My sister catches my left hand and gently pushes it down, and it's only then that I realize I was rubbing my eye again. "I know you're nervous," she says. "But it's okay. It's going to go great. I'll help you."

"I can do it myself," I say.

"I know you can. But I'm here, just in case."

When she heads for the stairwell, I follow.

Part of me hopes Jenna won't be home; maybe I won't have to deal with this conversation yet. But when Abby raps on the door, it opens right away, and there's Jenna with her warm, expectant smile. For a second I wonder if maybe she won't recognize me, if I'll have to introduce myself, but she says, "Hey, Sydney! What's up?"

"Hi," I say. "Is it okay if, um . . . Can we talk to you about something for a second?"

She swings the door wide. "Of course! Come on in." Then she turns to Abby. "Hi, you're Abbi, right? You did great at the debate."

"Oh my god, thanks!" My sister beams, glowing from the praise . . . and probably from being in Jenna's presence. It's impossible not to like Jenna instantly.

Abby steps into the room, then looks up and goes, *"Whoa,"* so I stop lurking in the doorway and follow. There are shiny silver stars and planets and comets hanging from fishing line all over the ceiling, some close to the plaster and others low enough to touch. They spin gently in the air from the vent and flash in the sun, sending sparks of light and arcs of shadow dancing all over the walls. They're so cool that my mouth drops open and I stand there gaping.

Jenna laughs. "Are they too much?" she asks. "Stella said it was okay to put them up—that's my roommate—but I'm not sure she actually likes them."

"No, they're . . . they're great. I love them," I say.

"They're amazing," Abby says. "I wish I had some in my room."

A cluster of stars catch the light all at the same time, and a flash of recognition shoots through me. Before I can stop myself, I'm saying, "Wait. Is that Cassiopeia?"

"Yes!" Jenna beams. "God, it took so much work to put them up in actual constellations, and you're the first one who's noticed."

"I'm not surprised she figured it out," Abby chimes in. "Syd loves astronomy. She's always reading books and watching videos about it."

I know she's trying to help me transition into the topic at hand; she probably thinks I'll feel better if I get it over with. But my heart was already going painfully fast, and her segue kicks it up another notch. I just need to stand here for another minute, breathing and taking stock of my surroundings and watching the reflected light of the stars move across Jenna's face.

But Jenna doesn't sense my need for silence. "Oh yeah? That's awesome. I had no idea you were into space stuff. You should come to one of our meetings sometime and look through our new telescope. It's *so* amazing. I mean, I know you're really busy with Committee stuff, but—"

She breaks off, a horrified expression on her face. She obviously knows what happened, and I hate that she knows. It doesn't seem like she thinks less of me, but she probably does. I don't see how she could *not*. I need to say what I came to say and get out of here before I humiliate myself.

I don't allow myself to think about the invitation to look through the telescope. I know she'll probably take it back in a minute.

"That's actually what I came to talk to you about," I say. "Committee stuff, I mean."

"Sure," Jenna says. She plops down on her bed and stares up at me, ready to listen.

I take a deep breath, like I taught Abby. "Vice Principal Rosenberg came to our meeting yesterday, and she looked at our budget, and . . . well, she saw the money I gave you guys for your trip to Cape Canaveral, and she said it was way too much and unfair to the other clubs, and . . . she's taking most of it away. There's not going to be enough left for even one person to go. I'm so, *so* sorry, and I feel completely awful about this, and—"

Jenna cuts me off before I can say *I understand if you hate me*. "That's okay," she says. "We knew it was a long shot. Honestly we were shocked when you said yes. None of us thought we'd actually get to go. It was just, like, a fun idea."

My whole body is braced for her anger, so it takes me a minute to comprehend what she just said. "Wait, what?"

"See? I told you she wouldn't be mad," says Abby.

"Of course I'm not mad," Jenna says. "I know it's not your fault."

"Oh." My muscles relax all at once, and I sit down hard on the other bed without even meaning to. "That's . . . Thank you."

"It would've been cool to have the tour, but we can watch the rocket launch online," Jenna says. "The NASA site streams all that stuff, and you can hear what mission control is saying and everything."

"I know," I say. "The NASA site is my homepage, and I've watched tons of rocket launches. That moment when the scaffolding falls away and those massive machines rise into the air like they've been waiting to break free—it gives me chills every time."

"Maybe we could set up a projector and watch it on a big screen somewhere," Jenna says. "That would be awesome. You should come watch with us."

She says it so casually, like it's a normal, everyday thing to say and not the sentence I've been hoping to hear for an entire year.

My instinct is to say *Really?* but I don't want to give her the opportunity to take it back. So I just say, "I would love that."

"Amazing," Jenna says. "I'll make sure you're on the emails when it happens."

If I were alone, this is the point at which I'd thank Jenna, stand up, and flee, happy to have secured the tiniest win. But Abby looks at me expectantly, and I know I have to be brave. If my sister could get over her stage fright and debate in front of the entire school, surely I can ask one question to one girl.

"Um," I say. "I was actually wondering—would you maybe have room in Astronomy Club for one more person? If I wanted to join and come to all the meetings? It's okay if you—"

"Of *course*!" Jenna says before I'm even done. I search her posture and her voice for signs that she's just agreeing because she's afraid of me or feels like she has to. But she's right on the edge of the bed, eyes bright, leaning slightly toward me. "There are only six of us—we'd *love* to have a new member. I have no idea why more people aren't obsessed with space. We meet every Thursday after class and sometimes at night if there's something cool to see. Ms. Wallander took us out last week and let us set up our telescope on the edge of the soccer field where there aren't so many lights. It was *the best*."

She keeps talking, her hands flying around in excited swoops, but I'm not listening anymore. My mind is full of images: Jenna and me side-by-side on the dark soccer field, taking turns with the telescope; Jenna and me at dinner, debating which planets in nearby galaxies are most likely to support intelligent life; Jenna and me sitting next to each other, staring open-mouthed with wonder as the SpaceX Dragon begins to fly.

We'll start with talking about space. I'll work hard and impress her with how much I know. And someday, if I do everything right, maybe we can talk about other stuff too. Maybe we can be real friends.

I've completely lost the thread of the conversation by the time Jenna stops talking, so I just say, "That sounds amazing," and she nods hard and says, "It *was*. Wait till you see."

"What's this?" Abby's over by Jenna's desk now, and she's holding up a black hardcover book with swirly silver designs in the corners. I recognize it without even reading the title.

"It's a Dungeon Master's Guide," I say, totally shocked. Josh has the same one, or at least he used to, when he and Dev and Antonia and I played. I haven't talked to any of them since I left for Brookside, so I don't know if they still meet up. Seeing the book conjures up the smell of Josh's basement— dust and laundry detergent and Cheetos—and the slightly sticky feel of the red Formica table where we used to do our campaigns.

I wait for Jenna to laugh at me for knowing something so nerdy, then say the book belongs to her roommate. But instead she breaks into a huge smile. "Oh my god, do you play?"

"Play what?" Abby asks.

"Dungeons and Dragons," I say. "Yeah. I mean, I used to."

"Do you want to join our group?" Jenna asks. "It's me and Annabelle and Kailani and Stella. I mean, you don't have to if you don't like it anymore. But we've been really wanting another person."

A wave of warmth sweeps through me, and I'm afraid my cheeks might be turning pink. This is different from Jenna letting me into her club when I asked. Now she's the one reaching out. Even if it's only because they want a fifth person, she doesn't mind the idea of the fifth person being me.

"No, I didn't stop because I didn't like it," I say. "I mean, I do like it. Yeah. I'd definitely play with you guys if you wanted." I don't want to come on too strong and scare her, so I keep my voice as level as I can. But saying the words makes me so giddy it's like I'm levitating slightly above the bed. "Are you the DM?"

"Yeah! Oh my god, this is the best. The other girls are going to be so excited. Abbi, do you play? You could both come."

"I don't even really understand what it is," my sister says, which is kind of weird, since I played for years. But I guess I never really explained it to her. I never explained much of anything to her.

"It's a role-playing game," Jenna says. "It takes place in this fantasy world. You each make up a character, and you go on quests together. Like fighting monsters or rescuing people or looking for treasure or whatever."

Abby wrinkles her nose. "Like improv?"

This is my chance to get her to say no, if I want; I know how Abby feels about improv. A few weeks ago—or even a few days, probably—I would've done anything to keep her from playing with us. But now I say, "It's not that much like improv. You make up your character's backstory and stuff, but the DM—that's the Dungeon Master, that's Jenna—she tells you most of the things that happen as you go through the quest, and you decide how you want your character to react. And some things are just chance—sometimes you roll dice to see what happens. You all figure out the story together."

Abby nods. "Yeah, okay. That sounds cool. I'll come."

"Amazing," Jenna says. She turns to me. "Who's your character?"

I think about my last D&D campaign: the way I suddenly changed my alignment to evil even though it benefitted nobody but me, the way I traded friendship and camaraderie for the ability to control everyone. Ruling through fear was effective, and it bought my character power and loyalty from everyone around her . . . until it didn't. When Josh and Dev and Antonia finally realized their characters were strong enough to overpower mine and banish her from the group, Capriana and I both ended up alone.

At the time, I refused to back down or say I was sorry, certain I hadn't done anything wrong. I was just playing the game, and there was no reason everything had to be fair. The rest of life certainly wasn't. But now, sitting in this room full of spinning silver stars and possibility, it seems like maybe there are other ways things could've gone.

"Syd?" says Jenna. My nickname rolls off her tongue easily, like she's known me forever.

I look up and meet her eyes, and when I smile, she beams right back at me, totally unguarded. "I used to play a rogue named Capriana," I tell her. "But I think I want to be somebody else this time."

199

About the Author

Alison Cherry is the author of the young adult novels *Red*, *For Real*, and *Look Both Ways* and the middle-grade novels *The Classy Crooks Club*, *Willows vs. Wolverines*, and *Ella Unleashed*. She is also the coauthor of *Best. Night. Ever.* and *The Pros of Cons*. She lives in Brooklyn with her cats.